Chicago Neighbors
A Year in Short Stories

Fr. Clete Kiley

Floricanto Press

Floricanto Press
7177 Walnut Canyon Rd.
Moorpark, California 93021

(415) 793-2662

www. *FloricantoPress*. com

ISBN-13: 9781099168765

"Por nuestra cultura hablarán nuestros libros. Our books shall speak for our culture."

Roberto Cabello-Argandoña and Leyla Namazie, Editors

Chicago Neighbors

Table of Contents

Preface   1

Acknowledgments   3

The Spirits of Women on a January Night   5

Apolinar   38

The Healing Arts   52

The Veneration of the Cross   63

Something Beautiful   78

Tres Pelos   94

The Tocayo   104

"Así Es La Vida"   119

El Grito de Dolores   136

Héctor's Dream House   154

Titi Belén   164

"I'll be Home for Christmas"   181

Meet some very interesting people. Meet their heritages. Watch them interact and push into promising futures of coincidence and cooperation. You will be richer for walking alongside these Chicago Neighbors. —**John Shea**, author of *Seeing Haloes*, (Liturgical Press)

"Clete Kiley has Chicago in his veins. It empowers his urban writing with character making his characters pop from the heart and memory. No disposable life here. All is sacred and worth savoring. In those little pieces, no matter how delicate or vulnerable, he's one writer with the brains to see the pathways leading to the bigger picture. Profound respect for the cross cultures in which we live, lets him lift up a truer America. Alive. Engaged. And ready for what lies ahead." . —**Thomas J. O'Gorman: Thomss J. O'Gorman is a writer and painter. The author of** *Frank Lloyd Wright's Chicago*, **and a weekly cultural columnist at** *Skyline Productions*.

Who is my neighbor? We all have wrestled with this perplexing question. Literally, who is my neighbor next door, across the street, in the apartment above, two streets down? We see one another, cross paths, breath the same air, and yet we seem to know little about those we call neighbors. Fr. Kiley' *Chicago Neighbors: A Year in Short Stories* serves as an antidote to the anonymity, sometimes distrust, that engulf us in fast-paced and often impersonal cities like Chicago, Los Angeles, New York. His stories reveal flesh-and-blood people who dream and hope, laugh and cry. The stories in Chicago Neighbors are a reminder that human existence is messy, complex yet beautiful, a crossroads where life and death meet, where the sacred and the sinful coincide in surprising ways. Take some time, meet Fr. Kiley's neighbors.

----- **Hosffman Ospino, PhD**, Professor of Theology and Education, Boston College

Preface

Chicago Neighbors: A year in short stories is meant to be a collection of epiphanies revealing God's presence and the way forward to becoming real communities. In these stories I hope to lift the joys, the hopes, and the anxieties and sorrows of immigrants and native-born folks interacting with each other. These interactions are experienced daily in many of Chicago's neighborhoods and Catholic parishes.

Epiphanies occur every day all around us wherever we live. Every day the people around us lift up glimpses of the meaning of human life. Every day the people around us, through their ups and downs, somehow manage to let us also get a glimpse of the divine. We believe God moves through human history and within human lives. Perhaps you will catch such a glimpse of God through one of my neighbors, or perhaps God will catch a glimpse of your truest self as you interact with these Chicago neighbors.

In the process of writing, characters simply step forward because they have something to say. Each of the characters in these stories are fictional, and has his or her own life, and experiences. Sometimes they take on names familiar. I think they thought if they used names familiar to me I might better pay attention to them in the writing process as they came to tell their story.

In these stories Mexicans and Puerto Ricans, and old Germans and Eastern Europeans, upwardly mobile professionals, first generation children of immigrants, immigrant families and same-sex couples, Catholic clergy and natively religious parishioners all collide in what we native Chicagoans might simply call: the neighborhood.

Today there is an ugly anti-immigrant rhetoric prevalent in our public discourse. Immigrants have always been a source of inspiration for me personally. They are and have long been a treasure to our nation. It is more important than ever to lift the beauty and the grace inherent in the encounter between immigrants and non-immigrants. I hope these stories will help foster such grace-filled encounters. I invite you now to spend a year with my Chicago neighbors. Welcome to the neighborhood.

Fr. Clete Kiley

Acknowledgments

Special thanks to my immigrant neighbors, to my colleagues in ministry and the people in the pews, to my UNITEHERE union members, and to Pope Francis—all for revealing the presence of God to me.

Thanks to Jack Shea for challenging me to write short stories; to Bosch Praisaengpetch for encouragement and help with this manuscript; to my family and friends who kept telling me to share these stories. And to the folks at Floricanto Press who made this book possible.

The Spirits of Women on a January Night

JANA AND DEBBIE HURST-DIXON WERE the first Lesbian couple to be married in a real church ceremony in Chicago by Pastor Julie Halvorson, herself the first openly Lesbian pastor at Christ's Redemption Church. Hundreds of guests attended the wedding, most invited, but others out to show support, some were just a little curious.

But this was only one among many firsts for both Jana and Debbie.

Jana was the first person, man or woman, to come out publicly in her small Catholic community in LaSalle county in west central Illinois. She was a senior in high school at the time. In another first, Jana was denied communion publicly by her pastor, Msgr. Wallace, in spite of her deep Catholic faith, in spite of the Catholic devotion of her mother, even though her German grandmothers and grandfathers had built St. Henry's Church with their own hands. Jana was the first Hurst not welcome.

Debbie Dixon was the first active duty member of her family in the U.S. military. She was the first to complete college, having done it in three years. She was a crack computer engineer and joined the Air Force right out of school. She was among those officers to first challenge the "Don't Ask, Don't Tell policy in the military.

They met each other several years ago at Big Chick's on Chicago's far north side on a Saturday afternoon after their women's softball game had been rained out in the final innings. Big Chick's was a great meeting place for all the LGBTQ community. But Saturdays especially, all the lesbian softball teams met at Big Chick's after the games for beers and free hot dogs. As such it was a great lesbian gathering place, one of the few really in Chicago, and every type of Lesbian was there from the frilly girly-types to the tattooed and pierced. There were a number who were just jocks, and enough resembled adolescent teen males so that an old gay man who drank away his Saturday afternoons at the corner of the bar, would look up hopefully from time to time, only to realize he was not looking at a handsome young man but a young woman,

"I am so confused" he would mumble.

That was where Debbie first spotted Jana. They exchanged numbers and had been together since.

But they continued their "firsts." They were among the first Lesbians to join an almost all Lesbian church. It was a church where women were the bishops, and pastors and mostly older gay men took care of the worship decorations and music. But it was a church that worked for those involved. Still, Debbie, who had never been raised religious in anyway, wasn't thrilled about getting involved. Jana was the one who was eager to join. In spite of her painful experience back home at St. Henry's, Jana was still deeply religious. This included devotion to the Virgin Mary, and saints, and all the "smoke and bells" as the gay sacristan called it.

Jana and Debbie were the first Lesbian couple to ask to be married in this new church. They were among their first friends to legally join and hyphenate their names. And they were the first again in their circle of friends to find a male donor suitable to both of them to donate so they could become pregnant. Jana insisted she wanted to carry the child. Debbie was okay with that. She wanted a child, too, but was not too excited about carrying one to term. The insemination took place in October and now as the New Year began Jana found herself with child.

But they found themselves in the middle of yet one more first: Jana and Debbie had taken the risk to open the first openly Lesbian business in their slowly gentrifying neighborhood. It was a book shop. It's focus on women: women authors, biographies of women, the Women's Movement, women's health, women's art, women's psychology, mothers and daughters, and relations between sisters. "We want to create a place that gathers the energy of women," Debbie told reporter from the neighborhood newspaper.

"There will not only be shelves of books, but an open space where women can gather, share, and empower each other." Jana added," there will also be special spaces for children to read, and interact. We want women, especially those who are care givers for children to be very much at home, and bring their children with them."

Debbie went on," We believe that women empower other women by sharing what we learn, what we read, what we experience. We hope that women will come here and do that for each other. You know, too often, our experiences are just dismissed, as though they mean nothing. We hope women will come here and know that their wisdom and experience is always honored." The reporter smiled wryly to herself as she noted the sounds of The Pointer Sisters coming from the store speakers: "Sisters are doing it for themselves."

Jana and Debbie planned for success, but they recognized it was still a risk: half of the neighborhood was still made up of Latino immigrants, another portion of old Germans and Eastern Europeans, and then also a slowly emerging population of Anglo college educated adults, and, of course, a growing LGBTQ community. As Debbie said to a doubting friend," Listen, every one of these communities is made up of more than half women. We have to find the right way to reach out and bring them in here."

Wisely they opened the book shop in October and with the focus on women, and the personal touches, like gift wrapping, they did very well over the holiday season.

On this bitter cold, but sunny, January day, they were re-doing the displays. "Where should we put the Gaia display?" Jana asked.

Debbie frowned at her. "You know that spiritual stuff is your thing." Things spiritual had come up between them periodically. But Jana had stressed that women were a great source of spirituality and not to include it in the store would be to ignore this gift.

"I'll pass on including church books and all that, but Debbie, there are lots of women into worship of the goddess today. Gaia is the book genre. And we probably should include some things from Wicca. Young women are looking for spiritual things today, but not the traditional religious stuff."

"Ok, but what are the crystals for?"

"Well, in ancient times supposedly women knew the healing power of crystals and herbs and other natural things. Let me just fix my little corner here, okay?"

"Well if you think the sisters will buy it, I 'll say okay. But we have to stay practical here, too."

"Jana, I have a call into Sandra Cisneros' publisher. I hope we can get her to stop by at the end of the month for that evening for Latinas. I mean the other writers are known, but she is from right here in Chicago from this neighborhood. I think if we can get the Latinas from this neighborhood in here to hear her, she would connect with them." This was part of a series of weekly women's conversations planned for the next three months.

"Oh, God, that would be wonderful," said Jana. "By the way I have the first flyers already printed up. I would make some rounds up the street here when I finish to the other shops to introduce myself and see if they would place them out."

"Oh, good idea. I'll watch the store."

"I thought I would go to Steinhauser's hardware store, and Michel the bread baker."

"What about that food and liquor store on the corner I'll bet that Puerto Rican lady there would take some or post them."

"Oh, yea, she is very sweet. Hey, I think I'll go to the church on the other corner. I wonder if they would put this out?" Jana wondered out loud.

Debbie had a look of disdain." Oh, Jana, it's a Catholic Church, "she almost hissed out." They're not exactly women friendly."

"I know, I know, but still it looks like a lot of women go there. Besides, Bobby and Jeff and some of their gay friends go there. They told me it is a pretty open place. They do all kinds of 12 step groups at that church, can you believe? They even have an S.A. group that meets there."

"But Catholics?" Debbie felt again for a bitter moment how much she detested organized religion, especially the Catholic religion. "I mean they are so anti-gay, anti –women, I mean how about anti-everything you and I stand for."

Knowing she would not win the argument on this count, Jana said, "Well, we have to see the women in that church as part of our market, don't we? They probably need us and the other women they might meet here." But Jana also thought to herself," God help me, but I do still love so much of it. And when Rocky is born (she called the child in her womb Rocky, for some reason) I think I will want to baptize him, if the priests will do it."

Jana buttoned up against the bitter cold and made her way to the various shops along Webster Street.

At each stop, she had been warmly welcomed by the shopkeepers, and each, in turn, gladly added the flyers to little racks by the front doors of their shops. Each shop was like a little community information kiosk.

Finally, she came to the church. It was an odd structure in the neighborhood. It's cornerstone said 1967. Every other building in the neighborhood was at least 60 years older. Jana tugged the door, but it would not give. Of course, it was locked. "How symbolic!" she thought.

Puzzled what to do, she looked next door at an imposing grey stone house. She noted immediately the capstone up near the roof that said 1893. A wrought iron fence seemed to link the modern church and the old house as aspects of one property.

"Guess I'll try next door," Jana thought, and then, *"Wow, is this house old! It must be one of the oldest in the neighborhood."*

But she was puzzled there was no sign to tell what this building was, but her gut told her: *"Rectory. This is the priests' house, I'll bet."*

This thought brought back some painful memories of St. Henry's back home. But summoning her courage she rang the bell. She waited. No answer. But she was sure she heard women's voices coming from the other side of the huge wooden door. She was sure it was women's voices, women's laughter.

She was about to ring again when the door opened, "Oh, I am so sorry to keep you waiting. Welcome to St. Monica. I'm Lupe Parra. Come on in."

Jana stepped into the hallway and her eyes immediately fell on a child, a girl of about three years old, astride a wooden rocking horse, grinning from ear to ear.

"Mama, mama, mira," the little girl shouted, "Look at me."

"Ooooh, *m'ija*, I see you," came a response in a woman's voice from a parlor off to the side of the hallway. There were more ooh's and aaah's from even more women from inside the parlor.

"Oh my God," thought Jana, *"This doesn't look like any Catholic church I remember."*

Lupe came back out of the parlor. "Well, have you been to St. Monica before?"

"No, I am still new to the neighborhood. My partner and I just opened a book shop down the street and…" she was interrupted by Lupe,

"Oh, yes, such a nice store! And all for women and children! I bought some Christmas gifts there last month. Oh, welcome, welcome to St. Monica.! I am one of the ministers here," Lupe said.

Jana thought to herself," A woman? A minister here? Did she say catholic?"

"Come in and say hello to our Latina ladies group. We meet every Thursday here. Ladies, senoritas," Lupe got their attention, and they all laughed at being called young women. "I want you to meet, Oh my God, I didn't even ask your name."

"Jana, Jana Hurst-Dixon."

"Ladies, this is Jana, she owns the book shop down the street, the one for women and children."

"Hi," a woman said very shyly, "you came to my store. So nice to see you. My name is Rosa."

"Well, I am Jana, oh, you have the food and liquor store, right? It's so nice to meet you. I just dropped off some flyers there before I came here. But there was a girl there."

"Yes, she's my daughter. She goes there after school, so I come here." Rosa smiled softly.

Jana was overwhelmed by the energy she felt in this place. "And a Catholic Church?" she wondered. It's supposed to be all dark wood and masculine.

"Lupe, I was hoping to drop off these flyers for the women, and maybe put some in the church. We are hosting an event at the end of the month for Latina women. We are bringing in Latina authors to the store, and I want to invite all the women to come."

The women grabbed up the flyers. "Do you have some more," asked Lupe. "We'll make sure the different parish groups get these two."

Jana was standing in the doorway between the parlor and the hallway when the huge front door opened. In stepped a man in a big puffy quilted ski jacket, gloves on his hands, hood pulled over his head, and his glasses steamed over.

"Oh my, it's getting seriously cold out there."

"*Hola, padre,*" said a few of the women. "Hello, Father."

Jana wondered looking back at the man as he unpeeled his winter coverings.

"*Hola, padre,*" again, and the little girl slid off the rocking horse and ran to hug the man.

"Fr. Tom, this is Jana, the lady with the book shop down the street." Said Lupe.

"Oh, what a pleasure to meet you," said Fr. Tom. Jana was still overcoming her surprise to see that the priest, after peeling off the outer wear was just dressed in a ski sweater and corduroys. "You have a wonderful book store."

"You mean you've been in Father?" asked Jana.

"Oh, the first week you opened. And I picked up a bunch of Christmas gifts, too. You have such a great selection. My nieces loved the books I got them."

Jana smiled, "Well, I am so glad to hear that."

"Oh, and the store is such a welcoming place," added the priest. "That is just the tone we are trying to set here, too."

Jana said," Well I came to drop off some flyers, but the women already took them all."

"Please bring some more, we'll be happy to put them out on our community board in the back of church."

"I don't know if Lupe invited you yet or not, but do you have a church you belong to?"

"Well my partner and I were married at Christ's Redemption. But we don't..."

"Oh, I know Pastor Halvorson. She is wonderful. So, are you Lutheran, then?"

"Well, Father, the truth be told," and she swallowed hard, "I am a recovering Catholic. No offense."

"None taken," replied the priest." You are always welcome here, if, or when that would ever make sense for you." And with a soft tone that indicated he knew a delicate situation, he added, "Your partner is also always welcome. But you are in good hands with Pastor Halvorson."

Jana was deeply touched, if not also a bit flabbergasted. She caught herself by surprise as she blurted out," Well, Father, one of these days I may need to get Rocky baptized."

She patted her stomach, and as the priest tried to figure out who Rocky was, Lupe, overhearing everything, shouted, "Oh, how wonderful" and gave Jana a warm embrace.

With that another parlor door opened and out came another group of people. Most averted their eyes and made their way through the group of women standing in the hallway and out the front door. But Jana heard from the back of the hallway, "Oh my God, Jana!" It was Bobby. "Are you signing up for the parish? I am telling you this is a wonderful place, wonderful people." Jana was delighted to see Bobby. He was always so full of energy, and Debbie was right," Bobby is as gay as it gets." Jana thought, "He is such a delightful queen."

"Father Tom, you met my friend, Jana?"

"Yes, we just had the pleasure."

The hallway was suddenly clogged with people. Carmen, the parish secretary and a very lively Puerto Rican, and, Jusha, the often dramatic Polish housekeeper came from the back of the house to greet everyone. There were lots of hugs and laughter. Jana saw that Bobby was amid all the hugs, and so was the priest. Meanwhile, she spotted a little boy who had been eyeing the empty wooden rocking horse, make his move. *"Mama, Mama, mira,"* he was shouting to his mother, but he was completely drowned out by the all the commotion.

And then something peculiar and rather extraordinary happened.

From within the parlor where the Latin women had been meeting, came a movement. The laughter and gossip of the women quieted, and the group seemed to part. And there in the middle of the hallway stood an old woman. She was very short, maybe five feet tall at most. She had dark brown skin, and black eyes. Her hair was silver and pulled back across the top of her head and woven into a single braid down her back. Around her neck she wore a large medallion with the image of the *Virgen* of Guadalupe on it.

Jana thought," She looks like one of those women from the Andes they show on National Geographic programs." But she was not chewing coca leaves, nor did she wear a derby hat. "But she must be indigenous- she is not just Latina," thought Jana. And despite her small stature Jana felt empowered by the presence of this woman. All the other woman had gone silent as well. Jana took that as deference for this diminutive lady.

"Ah, *Doña* Tomasa," said the priest, "*Bendición*." The wrinkled skin and severe look of the old woman's face broke into a smile,

"*Padre, bendición.*" She returned the courtesy.

There was a silence, that began to become uncomfortable for everybody, but *Doña* Tomasa simply stared directly at the priest, and, somehow, he had the good sense, or maybe the respect to wait for her to speak next.

"I have to tell you something, *Padre*. I have to tell you something," she repeated slowly. "Your house is haunted." Some of the women tittered nervously. "*Sí, padre*, you have a spirit in this house. Pay attention. She is a woman, *Padre*. I feel her. Don't ignore her, *Padre*. Before you go to sleep tonight, demand that she tell you her name. She must, *padre*."

"Well, *Doña* Tomasa, as we say in the creed at mass, 'God is the maker of all things, seen and unseen.' So, indeed we'll have to pay attention."

Doña Tomasa let out a very low, growling laugh, in a voice far too deep for her little body. On some days this laugh of hers annoyed the other women, but at this moment it rather frightened everybody.

Bobby broke the tension, "Father, you need to get a dog. They can always tell if there is a ghost in the house. But," and he paused mischievously," I wouldn't recommend a poodle." Jana burst out laughing, and she noticed so did the priest, and the staff.

"Well," Bobby added, "you know what they say: Beware of grown men with little dogs." He even amused himself with this additional retort.

But with no trace of humor, *Doña* Tomasa simply added, "*Sí, sí,* the animals know. But, *padre,* ask her yourself. Pay attention to her."

Back at the book shop Jana couldn't report fast enough on her visit to the rectory, the gathered women, the playing children, the welcoming priest, and, of course, *Doña* Tomasa. "Debbie, you never saw such a small person have so much power in a group of people. This *Doña* Tomasa was like right from the Aztecs or something. She is just fascinating."

"Weird," was all Debbie could muster which rather dashed Jana's excitement. Jana was hurt and went off to fuss at the display of crystals. "Look, Jana, I'm sorry. It's just all this religious stuff is so, I don't know, superstitious. And I hate to see women…I hate to see you get caught in it. Women have only gotten hurt from religion."

"Debbie, I'm not talking about religion. I'm talking about spirituality. I am talking about what intuition, and empathy, and second sight, and powers that women have had since the beginning of time. That is where our power is. I know you are an engineer. You are logical. But I am convinced women's power has been put down, and subjugated by logic. If we kill off our spirituality, we might as well kill off ourselves. At least, I might as well kill off myself."

"Jana, you know, I just wasn't raised around anything like this stuff. It makes me uncomfortable. And I don't want to see women written off because some man thinks we're flaky. And this stuff strikes me as flaky."

"But, Debbie, you are into women's empowerment."

"Yea."

"You have to meet this *Doña* Tomasa. She looks like a nobody. If she were on the street, we'd probably walk right past her. She is not particularly good looking. She is not dressed well. She has no degrees. I'd be surprised how much school she ever had. But this lady has power. I can't explain it."

"OK, that part, I'll grant you. But the ghost in the rectory part?"

"Look I don't know if there are ghosts or not, but you have to meet this lady."

Meanwhile the next morning at the rectory Fr. Tom just poured his first cup of coffee. Fr. Eddie Fealey, and Fr. George Kavunkal, priests from Ireland and India respectively, here in Chicago for graduate studies, joined him shortly. Finally, Jusha Lesniewska, the Polish housekeeper came in, followed by Carmen, the secretary, and Lupe Parra, the parish minister.

"Fr. Tom, did you hear what *Doña* Tomasa said yesterday about the ghost in this house?" Lupe posed.

"*Ay, Dio mío, Senol*, Jesu".

Carmen blessed herself to ward off some evil. Carmen had worked in the house for over twenty years since she had first come from Puerto Rico.

"*Padre*, it's true. *Es la verdad*. There's a ghost. "

"Well," said Fr, Tom, "we'll have to see."

"Oh no, Father, Carmen is right", chimed in Jusha. "We saw things right here in this kitchen."

"What things?", asked Fr. Tom.

Carmen excitedly said," doors open, the back door, the cabinets open."

Jusha interrupted," And a tray come flying across from that cabinet to the counter."

"And we hear footsteps on the back stairs here all the time," Carmen said pointing to the back-service stairs that ran from the kitchen to the three floors above.

"But I never heard of this before, ladies."

"Well, we didn't think you would believe us," said Carmen.

"Yes, we were afraid to tell you", added Jusha.

Fr. George rose from the table with a dramatic gesture, almost unfolding his six-foot frame.

"Fr. Tom, don't listen to these women. They are certifiable."

He dragged out this last word in rhythm with his Indian accent. He repeated," Certi-fi-able." He wagged his index finger disapprovingly, but without moving the rest of his hand.

But Fr. Eddie had a more ponderous look on his face, and said in his Galway accent, "Oh, now. Fr. George, that might be a bit harsh."

"Don't be telling me. Are you saying there is a ghost?"

"Well, I wouldn't say yes there is, but I wouldn't say no there isn't., George. And when they mentioned the back stairs here, well, I have to admit there's been a few nights when I thought we had a prowler in the house. I heard footsteps comin' up the back steps here. But I suppose I just put it out of my mind."

"Certi-fi-able," repeated Fr. George. "You are all certi-fi-able." And he stormed out of the kitchen.

A long pause of silence was interrupted when Fr. Tom said, "Well Bobby," and turning to Fr. Eddie and Lupe said, "You know of Bobby and Jeff across the street?...Well Bobby said maybe we should get a dog. Animals know."

"Oh, Fr. Tom, now don't be getting yourself a dog to prove you have a ghost. A dog will run you ragged, as if you don't have enough to do already. And don't be looking at me to walk the thing. I'm no good for the dogs."

"Ah, we'll see," said Fr. Tom. "*Doña* Tomasa did say to be sure to pay attention."

Two days later Jana and Debbie were in the book shop when they saw a man bundled up in a puffy ski jacket with the hood over his head, gloves on his hands, and being pulled along by a strange looking dog.

"Oh my God, I think that's the priest I met the other day."

"What is the thing on the leash?" asked Debbie.

"Yeah, that is one weird looking dog."

Fr. Tom saw the women in the window and waved. As he got to the door he opened it just a bit so as not to let the frigid January in.

"Thought I'd just say hi."

Jana said, "Father, come in for a minute and say hello to my partner, Debbie."

"Well, I've got my new charge with me and I'm not sure he's ready for your book shop yet."

The dog pulled and strained at the leash.

"But hi, Debbie, it's nice to meet you."

Debbie was staring at the dog. "What kind of dog is that, Reverend?" she asked with concern, but also deliberately using the term she knew was more familiar to Protestant ministers to keep the priest at bay.

She didn't look at him but stared at the dog. She was struck that the dog had pink eyes, and a wild look.

"They tell me he's an albino boxer. This is Aldo."

Jana smiled, "Hello, Aldo,." But the dog did seem wild.

"I thought he was a pit bull, Reverend."

"No, no, he's a boxer."

"Well you should get his ears clipped, then, so he looks like a boxer. I thought he was a pit bull."

Fr. Tom felt Debbie's hostility, even as he appreciated Jana's warmth. So, he decided to have some fun.

"Clip his ears, oh my God, I couldn't. The poor thing has been to the vet just twice; first they cut off his tail; the second time they cut off his balls. I couldn't see the poor thing hacked up any more. Right, Aldo," he said to the dog.

Debbie cracked a smile. "I see your point, Reverend. It looks like Aldo wants to continue his walk." The dog strained again at the leash. "Nice to meet you," Debbie said a little more cordially.

"See you both around. You've got a wonderful thing here."

Fr. Tom found both women a challenge, especially Debbie. But he decided these were women of integrity who owned truth as they knew it. He found himself admiring their courage.

"Okay. Come on, Aldo." He waved as he walked away.

"Boy, the last thing I ever thought I'd see in here was a Catholic priest!" said Debbie.

"He's been in before, Debbie- our first week."

"Really? I always wonder what these guys want."

"I know how you feel. Remember that's the world I grew up in. But he seems different to me. He's nice, really nice. I mean, he seems open. A lot of those guys are like put off by anybody different. Well, anyway, he's not like that Nazi priest back home. I kinda like him."

"Eh, we'll see. Jana, don't get your hopes up. I 'll kill him if he ever hurts you."

"That's why I love you," said Jana, and pecked Debbie on the cheek.

Back at the rectory, in spite of Fr. Tom's enthusiasm for Aldo, trouble was brewing.

One morning Aldo jumped at full height onto Fr. Eddie who was just about to pop a piece of toast into his mouth. Aldo growled and snatched the toast away in an instant.

"Aggressive little shite!" Fr. Eddie said under his breath. He acted angry, but, was quite terrified by the dog's behavior.

And then poor Fr. George came in late one night. Someone had inadvertently turned off the hallway light, so the house was pitch black. As he heard the front door lock behind him, and took a few steps into the hallway, he could hear the low growl, and finally, the pink eyes, which looked red at night. "Aldo, ha, ha. Aldo, oh, ha, ha," he repeated up the front steps to his room on the second floor. He sprinted the last few steps to his room and got the door between him and what he came to call "that certi-fi-able crazy dog from all hell."

Carmen was terrified of the dog, too, and so kept doggie treats in her pockets to toss to the dog to distract it as she went from the front parlor to the kitchen and back.

Of all the staff only Jusha seemed unafraid of Aldo. Quite to the contrary, Aldo seemed afraid of Jusha. She would stare at the dog and it was always Aldo who looked away first.

"*Nie dobre pies!*" "You bad dog!" "get out of my clean

kitchen!" "Don't you leave your guvna in my clean house, stupid dog!" This was her daily dialogue.

Jusha was what the Poles call a *"Gurala,"* or "Highlander" a term for people from the mountains to the south of Krakow. Animals were part of growing up, but they never had the run of somebody's house.

"You Americans are crazy" she would say to Carmen and Lupe, Puerto Rican and Mexican, "everybody here treats dogs and cats like babies. This is *glupje*, crazy. It's not the way God made the world to be. One of these days over here the pigs will be giving the orders."

Now somewhere around mid-January, after Aldo had been in the house a few weeks Jusha started a chain of events that led to tragedy.

Jusha had all the connections to be had in Chicago Polonia. She knew where to go for the best meat, the best sausage; where to go for a deal on a car, or on a fur. "Fr. Tom, you are very European, like me. You like nice things. You like to get good price, but best quality things. You are very European." That was Jusha's highest compliment.

On this particular day, Jusha told Fr. Tom, "Father, my friend called, the butcher. He just got some fresh ducks."

"Oh, for dinner, Jusha?" asked Fr. Tom relishing the prospect.

"No, no, Father, it's living ducks. But I take to my other friend and he fattens them up a couple of months. Then, it's good to cook. I must go over to pick up fresh duck now, or they will all be taken," she said as she raced out the door. "I'll finish cleaning later."

Jusha returned within the hour struggling with a large box.

Carmen held the back door for her as she came in with the box. "Carmen, I will take this upstairs to put in tub."

Carmen could hear the quacking of a duck. Jusha carried the box up the back stairs and headed toward one of the bathrooms on the second floor. That was when Aldo intercepted her. He had smelled the duck, and was growling, and barking, and lunged at the box in Jusha's arms.

"Shut up, you stupid dog!"

She put the duck in the bath tub, put in a dish of water and a head of lettuce, and slid the glass door closed.

Aldo was out in the hall growling and going wild. So, Fr. Tom took Aldo for a walk, but when they returned, Aldo broke away from him, and ran upstairs, and somehow barged the bathroom door open. The whole house heard the commotion. Jusha, Fr. Tom and Carmen all got to the bathroom at the same time. Aldo was standing at his full height, growling and howling and pawing the glass shower door. The poor duck was flapping his wings, quacking, and crapping all over the bathtub.

"*Nie dobre pies*, look what you're doing to my duck. You gonna give him heart attack.."

And with one swift movement she punted Aldo down the hall. Aldo growled at her intensely. But Jusha stood her ground, and Aldo began to piss all over the floor. He ran, yelping back to Fr. Tom's room.

"Okay, Fr. Tom, that stupid dog, he scare my duck. I got to take duck now to my friend. He's fatten up my duck if duck doesn't have a heart attack first. I'll clean bathroom when I come back. And, Father Tom, that dog is crazy!"

"Jusha, please. I don't appreciate that."

"You'll see, Father, everybody's scared of that dog. Not me, but everybody else. That dog is son of the devil."

Fr. Tom locked Aldo in his room, but the dog kept chewing on the carpet and the door jamb trying to get out and after the now long-gone duck. Finally, he locked Aldo in his bathroom, as far as he could get the dog from the scent of the dog. But still the dog growled and shook its head menacingly.

Later that night, about half past eleven, all the priests were coming back from different engagements and met in the front hallway. When they got to the second floor, they could hear water running, and feel steam in the air.

"Oh, no," said Fr. Tom." Don't tell me a radiator is broken."

Fr. Eddie thought to himself, "well, it is freezing out, and this house is old." But he said sympathetically, "oh, God, let's hope not",

Fr. Tom went into his room but came running out in seconds," Eddie, Eddie, Oh my God! The dog! The dog! Aldo! I think he's dead!"

Eddie went with Fr. Tom as they followed the sound of the running water. Eddie's blood ran cold when they entered the bathroom. The shower was running full blast. The water turned as hot as it could go. Steam filled the room. But there in the bottom of the tub was Aldo. Quite dead.

"He is dead, Eddie!"

And not meaning to be funny, but no friend of the dog, Fr. Eddie confirmed, "Sure he's dead as a door nail."

Fr. Tom was stricken. Fr. Eddie felt guilty for having wished the dog dead just days ago.

"Eddie, help me take him out."

"Sure. Where'll we go with him?"

"We'll have to bury him."

Eddie was puzzled and managed to interject," But, Tom, it's freezing out and the ground is frozen solid."

They carried the dead dog out to the alley, and seeing no alternative Eddie said, "Tom, we'll have to put him in here," pointing to the industrial dumpster behind the apartment building across the alley. "He'll have to go in, Tom."

"I suppose," said the resigned priest.

And over and in went the body of the dog. In the following days the neighborhood began to buzz with word of the dog's mysterious death. Some even said it was suicide.

"Dogs don't commit suicide," said Jusha when she heard it.

Toward the end of the month, at the book shop, the event for Latinas was getting underway. Unfortunately, to Jana and Debbie's disappointment, Sandra Cisneros was not able to come, but several other authors were planning to drop in. They were pleased with the turnout, though. The seats in the gathering place in the center of the shop were already filled. Many of the Latina ladies from St. Monica's were in attendance. *Doña* Tomasa was among them.

When she first entered the shop, she was quite drawn to the display of crystals. She began to touch, almost caress the stones. "*Oh, está bien,*" she said. She fingered one amethyst in particular, and then blessed herself with it.

Debbie watched the old woman suspiciously. "Is that Indian looking lady the one you told me about, Jana?"

"Yes, that's her," said Jana smiling. "You have to admit something is striking about her, Deb."

"I guess," Debbie said tentatively.

Jana watched *Doña* Tomasa place the amethyst crystal back in its place and take her place in a seat being held for her in the front row.

Jana could hear the ladies all talking about Fr. Tom's dog. "*¡Se suicidó!*" insisted one woman. "Dog's don't commit suicide countered another. "Oh, yes, but this one did."

Debbie turned to Jana," Are they talking about that weird dog the priest brought by here?"

"Yea, it died somehow right in the rectory.

"But did one of those ladies claim it committed suicide? I never heard of anything so goofy."

"I think that's what she said. My Spanish isn't that good."

"But that's ridiculous."

"Well apparently there is some mystery attached to it all. They say poor Father Tom is just crushed about it."

"Jana, why? C'mon, that dog was one weird beast."

"Pet parents, what can I say?"

Then, Jana and Debbie overheard two ladies arguing. "Oh, yes the *padre*'s dog did too commit suicide."

"No, no, no," answered back the other," La Polaca put a curse on that dog."

"*Sí, sí*", added another woman." The dog was jealous of her duck."

"*Ah, Dios mío*," responded the other woman back, and waved her hand in dismissal.

Debbie stepped to the front of the group, to end the chatter on the dog's alleged suicide and to get the program going. The authors, Latinas all, were going to talk about machismo in the Latino culture and how it crushed the spirit of women. Each writer spoke of her struggle to find her voice. One writer was a survivor of incest. She had strong words about the presence of incestuous fathers and uncles in the community. But her harshest words were for the mothers and grandmothers who looked the other way. Another endured a childhood plagued by a father's alcoholism and verbal abuse. Still another read a story about a hotel housekeeper's experience of sexual harassment daily.

Finally, that last speaker said, "Listen to the *machista* words of this old Mexican song: *El Rey*, which some consider the national anthem of *machismo*."

Writer Griselda Camacho went on, "*Con dinero o sin dinero, With money or without it, I do whatever I want. I have no throne, and no queen, and no one keeps me, but I remain the king.*" I think we have all seen enough of that. We Mexican women, we Latinas, need to fight for our voices."

Then she played a tape of a haunting song written by a local woman, Emma Nellie Gómez, called "*A Las Mujeres Liberadas.*" She explained that Emma Nellie wrote this song as a direct rebuttal to machismo, but also as a direct result of a beating from her husband.

The bilingual discussion following touched on many themes and eventually came to the issue of women and their spiritual power. This was the part of the program Lupe Parra was waiting to get to. She was a great believer in the spiritual power of women. That is what brought her to church ministry. But she was a bit jarred when Griselda Camacho made the statement, "Women's spirituality needs to be de-constructed from religion altogether! Religion has only oppressed women from the beginning." Griselda was certainly not here to dialogue about this. But Lupe wasn't going to sit for this,

"What about the great saints, like Teresa of Ávila, or even our Saint Monica. They had enormous influence. What about Mother Teresa?."

"But there are no women popes are there?" retorted Griselda rather condescendingly.

"What about the Inquisition? Burning of women as witches? Bundling strong women off to monasteries?"

The dialogue was getting heated and going nowhere so Jana interjected, with a slight nod to *Doña* Tomasa, "Let me ask about the spiritual power women have in the indigenous cultures that make up the Latina world. Griselda Camacho was about to offer another apodictic comment, but the whole room looked toward *Doña* Tomasa. She sat serenely, adjusting her rebozo, and stroking her singular long gray braid. But she said nothing. The room filled with a long pregnant pause.

Doña Tomasa lifted out from under her *rebozo* a large medallion of the Virgin of Guadalupe. Finally, *Doña* Tomasa spoke, "Look at her. Who does the woman look like?" she pointed to the image on the medal.

"Our people were conquered, but does she look like the queen of Spain?" She held the image so each woman could look on it.

"No, she looks like me, like our people, but the *gachupines*, bow down to her. So, which one has the power? And staring at Griselda fiercely she asked, "Does she look like a pope, or the priests you worry about? "and after a pause she went on, "No, she looks like all of us. So, who has the spiritual power?" She did not take her gaze from Griselda Camacho. The silence in the shop was dramatic.

"She is Tonantzín, the mother, the Protector. We go to her because *ella es la curandera*. We bring to her our sick. For good luck, or to ward off evil, we go to her."

"You talk about the *machistas*, but why do you give away your power to them?"she looked at each of the writers who had spoken with no sympathy on her part. Still holding the medallion she went on, "The bishop at Tepeyac and all the priests since then submit to her. Yes, men are *machista*. They are too proud, and they think they can control everybody, yes," pointing to one of the writers," you are right, they think they can control even our bodies. But she is everywhere, and in the end, even the *machistas* break down and die. And then they are afraid."

"Look at her. She is stepping on the devil here, and no men, not even the *brujos* can defeat her. You think an evil father can defeat her? They fear her." She aimed this at the writer who had spoken about incest. And to the one who spoke of an abusive and alcoholic father, she directed these words, "Do you think some *borracho sucio* can defeat her? No, never."

"But *Doña* Tomasa," Debbie decided to insert herself. This was getting all a little too Catholic for her taste. "The Catholic Church oppresses women. At least some churches embrace the gifts of women better.

Again, there was a long silence, and *Doña* Tomasa spoke, "You know nothing."

Debbie's jaw dropped, "Now just…"

Doña Tomasa kept on speaking, "She uses the church to make men behave."

"So, wait a minute, let me get this straight: the Catholic Church is a feminist conspiracy to control men?"

Debbie persisted, and again in a condescending way which began to offend the Latinas, even the writers.

"You worry about all the wrong things. You act like men and think you can control everything. You cannot! Tonantzin knows that. She is the mother. She knows the flow of everything, of all the things in nature. She does not try to control them. She works with them. Pay attention to yourself, to your woman's heart. Be like her. You will see the world as it is. It is spiritual. And women can see the nature of things. Women see what men cannot see. The hidden ways in all things. But you women doubt," she said pointing to the writers, and turning back to Debbie. "You doubt your power, so you think you have to act powerful like men. But men cannot heal. They cannot protect the people. They submit to her. She is the power of women."

One of the ladies from Saint Monica could not resist, "*Doña* Tomasa, what about the *padre's* dog? Did it commit suicide like some people think?"

Another lady added, "*Doña* Tomasa, you were the one who told the priest to get a dog, no?"

Again, a long silence. "No," I told the priest there was a ghost in his house and to pay attention to her."

Debbie rolled her eyes, and whispered to Jana, "Not that damn dog again!"

"It was our friend Bobby who suggested the priest get a dog to see if there was ghost in the house," said Jana, to Debbie's annoyance.

Doña Tomasa sat again for a long pause. Then her cackle cut the silence like a knife. "That dog did not commit suicide. She had to protect the priest and all the children who go to that house. She killed that dog."

"Oh, for Chrissake," whispered Debbie. But even the Latina writers were now riveted.

"The spirit of the woman heals and protects. It is the brujos that manipulate the animals. The minute I saw that dog, I knew. That dog had a spirit in it. It came from the *brujos*. It frightened the people, and those woman at the church," she nodded at Lupe Parra, "and, I think, even the priests. It was going to attack someone very soon. So, she killed it. Those priests are lucky to have her. I told him to pay attention to her."

Griselda Camacho had to admit, in spite of her earlier dismissal of her, she was becoming fascinated by this old woman. "So how did you know the ghost was a woman?"

"I felt her presence. All of you could, but you doubt yourself."

Lupe Parra decided to tell what she knew about the rest of this tale.

"*Doña* Tomasa, you told Fr. Tom to pay attention to her. And he did. You told him to demand she tell her name when he went to sleep." *Doña* Tomasa turned toward Lupe and smiled but said nothing.

" What happened, Lupe?" came a chorus of voices.

"Fr. Tom and the other priest, from Ireland, Fr. Eddie, did what you told them, *Doña*. They told the ghost she must tell them her name when they would sleep. I couldn't believe it. But I was there when they told what happened. Fr. Tom said she said her name was Gathri.. or something like that. But Fr. Eddie said her name was Ella. But it didn't make any sense to us. But later on, Mary and Cecilia Claus were in the rectory. Mary is 90 and Cecilia is 89 and they have been living here their whole lives. So, Fr. Tom asked them if they ever remembered an old parishioner named Gathri, or Ella. He wondered if there may have been an old housekeeper or somebody they remembered."

"Mary Claus just shook her head,"

No, I don't remember those names."

But Cecilia said, "Mary, do you think he means Gabriella Meyerhoff?"

You should have seen Fr. Tom's face when he heard that.

"Gabriella Meyerhoff? Who was she?"

In tandem the Claus sisters started talking, "She was the old German housekeeper here. She taught us how to use the mangle. We would help her do the church linens. Oh, Father, you could have eaten of the floors in this house it was so clean. Oh, father, she used to protect the priests so much, and when kids would be playing out around the house she would chase them away shouting, 'The priests are having a rest. Geht aus! Ruhe!'"

Lupe concluded, "So, *Doña* Tomasa, it looks like you were right. It was a she and she did protect that house."

"I told the priest to pay attention. Now I tell you women" and she held up the medallion again, "Pay attention to her, if you want to have power."

After everyone had left the shop, and after the doors were locked up. Jana said to Debbie, "Wow, what a night! I mean talk about the spirits of women warming a January night! You couldn't bring all these different pieces together in a million years."

"Jana, women are wonderfully complicated, aren't we? There is always another layer. But you know what struck me was that old *Doña* Tomasa woman. I thought she was pretty out there, I have to admit. I am not kidding, like someone from up in the Amazon or someplace. But when she said we doubt ourselves, our power...when we act like men and try to out power them at their own game...wow...something to think about. I am not into her medallion and all that Catholic juju, but..."

"Yeah, but, you can't beat the spirits of women on a January night".

Apolinar

TONY HERNÁNDEZ FIRST MET APOLINAR Vega in the bus terminal in Cuernavaca as they both waited for the Flecha Amarilla bus to re-board and take them north through Mexico City and on towards the border at Matamoros and Brownsville. Tony was still called Tonio at that point. He had left his rancho in the shadow of the two volcanoes, Popo and Ixti near Puebla, the day before. He picked up some coffee and pan dulce and was walking back to his departure gate when he spotted Apolinar. Tonio said to himself, "*Ay caray, that guy looks like Emiliano Zapata.*"

Indeed the man did. He was short in stature, probably middle–aged, with dark brown skin, jet black hair, and almond shaped black eyes. But unlike Zapata, Tonio thought, "*es más indito*", "He is even more Indian." Tonio was always outgoing so he sat down next to the man and offered him one of his *panes dulces*.

"*¿Vas al Norte?*" Tonio asked.

"*Sí, pues*", the man answered.

"Yes, me, too. I am going to Chicago. How about you? Where are you headed?" Tonio asked.

The man simply said, "*Pienso irme a Mexico*".

38

Tonio thought he detected a faint accent in the man's Spanish. Tonio thought to himself, "*I'll bet this man doesn't speak Spanish at home very much.*"

He continued intrigued. "I am going to meet my brother, Hermilo in Chicago. Do you have someone waiting for you in Mexico?"

The man answered simply once again, "*No, pues*".

"You mean you're going alone, and nobody over there waiting for you? Do you know Mexico?" he asked the man, adding, "it's such a big city, you can get lost easy. I was there once before. Have you been there?"

Again the man responded, "*No, pues*".

"But why do you want to go, *hermano*?"

After a long silence the man finally responded.

"In my village we have no work. Before I was un *azucarero*, you know, I cut the sugar cane. But now there's no work. I have my wife and my children there, but what kind of a father cannot feed his family? So, I have to go."

Tonio liked this man. He struck him as a gentle soul, and he wanted to help.

"Same for me", said Tonio. "That's why I am heading *al Norte*. There is no work near *mi rancho* either. I have three children, too. I have to leave to find work to support them. But my brother, Hermilo, he went over five years ago. He married a Tejana and moved to Chicago. Now he has a baby, a green card, a *camioneta* and a job. *Ya es casi un gringo*", Tonio added and started to laugh. "He told me, 'If you can come over there is a job for you in Chicago.' So I am going to Chicago. They got a lot of jobs over there. Hermilo told me, they even have jobs for those who *andan mojados*."

"*Mojados*?" Apolinar was puzzled at the meaning of the term, "those who walk around wet."

"Oh, it means *sin papeles*. I don't have any documents to let me into America. So, we have to swim across el Rio Bravo. So, we get wet." He laughed. So did Apolinar.

Apolinar sat pensive for a while then with a stoic composure, "Is Chicago near Mexico?" he asked.

"*Ay. Caray, no*," said Tonio. "*Está muy lejos*. It is way up in the north and Hermilo told me it gets very cold there. But he said you learn to live with the cold. Maybe that's why there are jobs there, because it is too cold."

"Then I will go to Chicago," said Apolinar.

"But you don't have anybody over there. It could be dangerous for you."

"I'll go with you to Chicago."

"Ok, why not, but what is your name?"

"Apolinar Vega. I come from Tepozteco. It is not far from here."

"Antonio Hernández from Rancho Cruces near Puebla, *a tus* órdenes", said Tonio as he reached out to shake Apolinar's hand.

"Are you sure you don't want some of this *pan dulce*."

Apolinar was grateful for the food. He had not eaten in two days.

"That was two years ago," thought Tonio, now called Tony Miller, to match the name on his social security card and his drivers' license. He marveled at all the time passed since he and Apolinar crossed the river into Texas, and hitched rides and took buses north to Chicago. On the journey they had come to rely upon each other. When they arrived they moved into Hermilo's house. Tony lived upstairs with his brother and his family. Apolinar was given a curtained off portion of the basement. They both got jobs through Hermilo's *compadre*. It was menial work, sweeping up in a factory. They worked the second shift which was lucky for them because the day La Migra raided the factory, it was done during the first shift. But it was unlucky because the Jefe called Hermilo's *compadre* to tell him to tell Tony and Apolinar not to come to work anymore. Things were too risky.

Soon Tony got work in a factory making false teeth. It was a dingy place on Chicago's lower west side, but in the barrio Mexicano, and not too far from Hermilo's house. Apolinar got a job as a busboy and a dishwasher in a Greek restaurant. His days were long and hard and paid very little. But when he could, he would have Hermilo take him to Western Union to send money to his father in Tepozteco.

Tony used to tease Apolinar.

"Hombre, you are too *Indito* in your ways. People think you are too *humilde* and they can push you around."

Indeed, Apolinar had a demeanor that could be mistaken as meek, *"humilde,"* but it was the quiet and stoic way of his people.

"They're gonna bully you, man," Hermilo chimed in on more than one occasion. "You need to stand up to them."

But Hermilo and Tony, and the other Mexican men used to tease Apolinar especially because his boss at work was a woman.

One night after all of them had had too many *cervezas*, Apolinar swore to them, *"Jamás, nunca voy a trabajar para una mujer*; I will never work for a woman anymore." And he never returned to that job.

In the Fall, he had been doing some landscaping, but with the on-set of winter that work went away. He got some odd jobs painting, but nothing regular, and, in fact, he was not much of a painter. The fact was there was no job, no money. He had not sent anything to his wife, Salinas, in months. He could offer nothing to Hermilo and Tony for the space in their home, nor for the meals in which they now included him. He was having a hard time of it. He felt ashamed, and utterly alone. He kept hearing a Mexican *ranchera* song on the radio about Guanajuato with a chorus that brought home the message: *"donde no vale la vida, donde la vida no vale nada*; where they do not value life, where life is worth nothing."

"That is my life here in Chicago. That is my life in Tepozteco. *Mi vida no vale nada. No me tienen respeto.*"

This had become *'la lucha'* each day for Apolinar. He was a man, but he felt no one held him in respect.

February in Chicago is always cold. This night was no exception. The cold and damp just penetrated even the warmest clothes. Chicago's short winter days had been gray all week. As winter night once again settled, Apolinar Vega felt the loneliness and sadness once again taking his spirit. He was a man in a cold dark country with no documents, with no family near him, and once again with no work. As he lay on his cot in the corner of the basement, Apolinar was nostalgic. His reverie took him back to his boyhood in Tepozteco, a small indigenous village that clung to a mountain ridge overlooking the valley of Tepotzlan, in Morelos, Mexico. His memories swirled and he began to dose off and dream. His dreams brought images of his father, a small man with dark brown skin, and jet black hair, with almond shaped eyes and a stoic demeanor. He saw his mother, her colorful skirt and a rebozo over her shoulders; her braided black hair; her shy smile. He heard them speak to him in Nahuatl, but he could not understand what they were saying. His wife, Salinas was standing behind them, holding a baby. She said nothing and seemed to look away.

"Is she ashamed? Of me? Why does it give her la pena to look at me? Does she have shame? Did she betray me?" These were the thoughts that troubled Apolinar awaking in a groggy fog.

"Apolinar, *vámonos".*

Apolinar woke from his grogginess with a start as he heard Tony calling him.

"Apolinar, hombre, ya nos vamos al cumpleaños de Carolina".

"Ay, sí", Apolinar remembered.

They were all invited by *Doña* Clotilde to celebrate her daughter Carolina's 26th birthday.

"*¡Ahorita, voy!*" Apolinar shouted to Tony.

But Apolinar did not move. His dream haunted him. And dreams were something taken very seriously by his indigenous community in Tepozteco. His father and mother and his wife had come for a reason which he could not yet divine. All he could say to himself was, "*Yo me siento tan mal*", "*I feel so bad.*"

As he straightened out his bed, Apolinar stopped in mid-action. He stood erect and said to himself, "*Ya me voy*", "I've got to go." And he was not referring to Carolina's birthday party. In that moment he knew he had to go home — to Tepozteco — with no fortune, with no brave tales to tell, a failure, a man who had earned no respect. The pain of that knowledge cut his heart like a machete. But Apolinar was *un Indito*, not a sentimental Mexican. Like his father before him he learned a man carries such pain with a stoic heart. "*Es mi destino. I will go*", he thought.

But *Doña* Clotilde sensed some months back that Apolinar was lost. She did not know Apolinar's village or his people, but she knew enough that his reactions would not be the same as she might expect from other Mexicans. His was another culture. His people were poor but among those things they valued more than anything else was the order of respect within the family. And while Apolinar was not finding any success in Chicago, there was always more to him. *Doña*

Clotilde saw something deeper. She saw him as a courageous man, a husband and father, who had risked everything to cross over to America, who suffered brutal Chicago winters, and the loneliness of having no family or others from his people here. She saw him as a man who bore his difficulties stoically. *"Pero, ya está harto,"* she thought. *"He is at the end of his rope."* Her intuition told her he had lost face with the other men. And she could see the other men would pretend otherwise, but they too had given up on Apolinar. She knew he would one day just up and leave. She felt that day would be soon. So, she invented the excuse of a party for Carolina's birthday, but in her mind it would also be a farewell for Apolinar. She quickly passed the word to *Padre* Lorenzo, and to the members of the Mexican choir to come to her house this night.

When Tony had first suggested to Apolinar they join Fr. Lorenzo's choir, it seemed like a good idea to him. Tony had a beautiful voice and loved to sing. So did his brother, Hermilo. Apolinar could not carry a note. But he liked the *Padre*, and the group always seemed to have a good time. Besides the choir brought out a group of *guapitas*, attractive women, and seemed to be a safe place from the Migra.

On top of that, *Doña* Clotilde was the energy behind it all. She had become the surrogate mother and grandmother for this whole group of immigrants so far away from home. For the young women who came to the choir she provided a needed chaperone for the benefit of over protective fathers, or uncles. And she reminded Fr. Lorenzo more than once now, *"Padre, tú y yo, somos los buscanovios,* we are the matchmakers for these couples."

Everyone gathered at *Doña* Clotilde's bungalow, as these houses were called in Chicago. Her son-in-law, Poncho, passed out more beers. Ángeles and the other women set out guacamole and fritos. The beers made the men feel warm in spite of the cold weather outside. Tony, Hermilo and Apolinar arrived last. And everyone laughed when they came in with their heads wrapped with scarves only revealing their eyes.

"*Ya parecen terroristas*", shouted Martín Galván, the choir director.

But Clotilde dismissed his statement saying, "they had to protect their voices."

Everyone laughed again.

Shortly Tony began to sing a haunting song called "*Flor Silvestre*" about a simple country flower from the woods high on a mountainside to be preferred to roses or lilies.

Gabriel then took the guitar and began to sing the *Canción Mixteca*, a song reminiscent of the indigenous songs of Mexico. He sang,

> "*O tierra del sol, land of the sun, suspiro por verte; I long to see you; I live so far away, without light, without love. I see myself alone, so sad, like a leaf in the wind. Immense nostalgia fills my heart; I want to cry, to die, of sentiment.*"

Everyone joined in the chorus. Hearts were full. *Doña* Clotilde looked over at Apolinar. He sat with that usual stoic look, but she saw in his eyes something else: determination.

Soon everyone was busy telling *chistes*, jokes they had all heard a hundred times before, but were always hilarious in the re-telling, amidst the many comments from the sidelines. The *chistes* broke the mood of Gabriel's song. And Clotilde noticed that Apolinar had joined in the joke telling, and his jokes were getting the loudest laughs.

Clotilde, Carolina, and the other women set out plates and cups and then with a great flair brought out a large *Tres Leches* cake and put it on the table. To Apolinar's surprise, it was not a birthday cake, but on it made of frosting was his name, and an eagle and a nopal cactus. The message read: "*Apolinar Nuestro Amigo*", "Apolinar, our friend." Everyone clapped for Apolinar. There were *abrazos* and a few tears.

Eduviges, clowning around until he got everyone's attention, said, "I have a presentation to make on behalf of the choir." He went on, "Apolinar, tonight we want to honor you because of your great voice!"

The entire room erupted in laughter, and so did Apolinar.

"But *Don* Martín told me the best thing for me in this choir was not to sing at all," said Apolinar.

Everyone laughed again.

Eduviges continued, "Apolinar, seriously, we want to thank you for your friendship. You remind us all of where we come from. Maybe you are the person '*más Mexicano*' in this group. We know *La Lucha* has not been easy for you here.

But we respect your simple way, the way you remind us all of our families back in Mexico. And so we wanted to make this Apolinar night in Chicago."

It was all rather overstated, and everyone knew it, so did Apolinar, but it was the Mexican way. Apolinar thought, *"Nunca en mi vida, never in my life, have I been honored like this."* His determination to return to Tepozteco was now confirmed and blessed in this gathering.

About two weeks after the party, Apolinar returned to Tepozteco. No one heard anything from him nor about him for more than six months.

One day while working at the tooth factory some new men were brought in, and one of them was seated next to Tony.

"Tony, show this guy the ropes, ok? He don't speak no English at all, and I'm not so sure about his Spanish", said the manager.

Tony got the gist of the request and turned to look at the man.

"*Ay, caray*", Tony said to the man, expressing his surprise, "you remind me of an old friend of mine. What is your name?"

"Heriberto Sánchez", the man responded.

"*¿Usted es Mexicano?*" Tony asked.

"*Sí, ciento por ciento,*" answered Heriberto, "*del estado de Morelos.*"

"*Hey, mi amigo* is from there. But he went back. His *pueblo* is called Tepozteco, do you know it?"

The new man lit up at the mention of the name, "*O, sí, sí,* I come from Tepotzlan. It is the valley below Tepozteco."

"Well, maybe you know my friend. His name is Apolinar Vega," Tony asked excited at the prospect of hearing news of Apolinar.

Heriberto did not disappoint Tony. He did know of Apolinar and told a tale that made Tony's hair stand on end. He knew he had to call Hermilo right away.

"Hermilo," he called his brother, "we need to go to the choir tonight. I heard about Apolinar. No vas a creer! You won't believe it!""

That night as the choir gathered for practice, Tony recounted what he had heard about Apolinar. His tale shocked them all. He ended reporting that Apolinar was being held even now in jail for murder. *Doña* Clotilde begged, "Hermilo, tell us what happened."

"Pues, this new guy came to work with us, and he is from the town just below Apolinar's pueblo. He says that when Apolinar got back to his home, his friends came to greet him. They thought he must have come a wealthy man after these years. But it was soon apparent that Apolinar had not had success. He was still a poor man. '*Es su destino*', the old men in town said. There was resignation and pity in their voices. The women looked to their husbands for cues how to receive Apolinar home, and wondered how they could help his wife, Salinas, bear up with this. It was awkward for everyone."

Tony went on with the tale. "But then, his *compadres*, Luis and Yolanda Ayala came by. They had come by to welcome him home. But Luis had come to tell Apolinar he got a job for him in the sugar refinery. But there were other things Luis had to tell Apolinar, that had to be attended to first. Luis was loyal to his *compadre* and knew he had to tell him about a young sugar cane cutter who had been paying too much attention to Salinas while Apolinar was away in America.

But Tony went on, "How do you tell your friend about un engaño, a betrayal? Pues, according to this Heriberto, Luis and Apolinar went to a *cantina* for a few beers, but once they got to the *cantina*, Luis ordered tequila instead. '*Compadre*, he said, and out came a few jokes, the job offer, and an update on life in Tepoztec, and a hundred questions about life in Chicago, and how Apolinar had come to arrive there. *Pues*, they lost count of all the tequilas, then Luis got down to telling Apolinar about the sugar cane cutter named Rafael. Luis told him, '*compadre*, this Rafael was paying attention to Salinas in the *mercado* on Sunday afternoons after the *misa*. I tried to watch out for your honor. But you know how it is when a man wants something. So then Apolinar is supposed to have shouted: '¡*Engaño! Traición!*' You know there can't be anything worse, right?"

Everyone was on the edge of their seats as Tony continued, "So, this Luis told Apolinar: 'don't blame Salinas. You can't blame women. When a man is strong, *compadre*. Well, you know. But mi *comadre* is a good woman. She told him to leave her alone.' But rage filled Apolinar. He went home and kicked in the door of the house. '*Puta, que me hiciste cabrón*; whore that made a goat of me.' Apolinar, gentle Apolinar, beat up his wife."

50

As Tony said this the group gasped. None louder than *Doña* Clotilde.

"But wait," Tony said, "*hay más*, there is more. Three days later, Apolinar waited in the darkness outside the *cantina* for that cane cutter named Rafael. When Rafael emerged somewhat drunk, Apolinar walked up to him. He looked him in the face and nodded slightly to him. Rafael was *borracho*, so he stopped, and looked at Apolinar again. They said the man recognized Apolinar for a moment and he was about to say something. But without any words, and as quick as he could, Apolinar slashed the man's head almost half off his shoulders with his cane cutting machete. And when the body fell to the ground, Apolinar cut the head off completely."

Doña Clotilde and the other women sat completely horrified and said nothing.

But in the voices of the men, if one listened carefully, beyond the sense of shock, there was something else: a sense of admiration.

Tony finished the story telling the group Apolinar was in jail for the moment, but was not expected to be there for long.

"After all, how could a man be blamed for defending the honor of his wife and family?"

The women continued to sit in horror as they heard Tony say this. So did those who had lived some time in Chicago.

But whenever Tony and his brother, Hermilo, and the other men want to convey to their sons what a real man of honor is they repeat this story and tell their sons to "Remember Apolinar. That was a man of respect."

The Healing Arts

LA BOTÁNICA SAN LÁZARO SEEMED out of place as the Logan Square neighborhood was slowly gentrifying. But there it was just as it had been since 1960 when Beatriz Soto first opened it after she arrived from Puerto Rico. Its shelves were stocked with blessed *candelas*, incense, sage, and lotions-lotions for good health, for love, for sexual prowess, or to ward off mal de ojo or other negative spiritual forces. Rows of plaster statues filled one whole wall. In another aisle there were glass cases with herbs and roots of every kind.

Although she had come from Mexico herself, *Doña* Cuca Espinoza felt at home in this little shop. She always nodded to each of the santos, many were old friends, as she made her way down the aisle. But today she needed a remedy very badly and she made her way to the cases of herbs looking for something familiar and hoping Beatriz had it in stock.

March is a cold and damp month in Chicago. At 82 years of age, *Doña* Cuca was a very mobile woman. She walked miles every day and was amazingly spry. But in March the cold and damp weather took a toll and her knees ached and were swollen every morning when she awoke.

"*Ah, es mi artritis,*" she would say as she hobbled for the beginning of each March day. It took until noon most days for her knees to loosen up enough for a good walk.

"I need to find *mi popote,*" she told her neighbor.

"*Popote?* What's *popote?,*" asked Mary Hernández, her neighbor.

"Oh, it's the *yerbas,* you know the leaves to make a plaster. For my knees," she explained rubbing her knees. "My *artritis. Ay,* it hurts too much this month. Mary, do you know where I can get mi *popote?*"

"Cuca, I don't know what that is." She turned to her husband Joe, who was coming down the front steps with their son, Ralphie. "Joe, did you ever hear of *popote? Doña* Cuca is looking to get some. It is some herb for arthritis."

"*Popote?* Never heard of that, Cuca," said Joe Hernández.

Ralphie just listened to this back and forth, and then he showed a puzzled look. And then seemed to answer his question.

"Well, I'll go to the Botánica San Lázaro to see if they have it," said Cuca.

On her way, she neared the book shop, stopped, looked in, and spotted Jana. Cuca lifted the amethyst crystal on the chain around her neck that she recently bought from Jana, the shop owner. She caught Jana's eye, dangled the crystal, and walked on. Cuca was very happy with this treasured amulet.

Entering the Botánica San Lazaro, Cuca stopped to look at a new statue of San Judas Tadeo. He was the saint for lost causes. He was popular with women whose husbands were hopeless alcoholics, and for those who were desperate that they would never find a new boyfriend or girlfriend. But he was also the saint to go to when someone's situation was just dire: no money, no job, no family, or near death. Cuca kissed the tips of her fingers and touched San Judas on the head. To Cuca these were not just statues. A *santo* was a real person with whom one had a real relationship. They became part of one's family, like an aunt or uncle. They always had to be treated with respect.

"*Oye, San Judas, ayúdame encontrar mi popote*", Cuca whispered. "St. Jude, help me find my *popote*."

Beatriz Soto watched the old lady with pleasure. She liked to see her clients treat her *santos* this way. She saw them as her family members as well. And to sell a statue to someone was not an exchange of merchandise, but more like betrothing a member of your family to someone else's.

"*Hola, Beatriz*," Cuca began, "I am looking for mi *popote*. I see all the remedies here, but do you sell *popote*? My *artritis* is too much, and I need to make a plaster."

"*Popote*? Cuca, I never heard of *popote*. What is it? Is it Mexican? Maybe one of those *yerbas de los los inditos*?

"*Sí, es una yerba*. It's the weed that grows wild. We call it *popote*. In Mexico, *las Viejas* make a plaster from it, and, ooh, it always make you feel a lot better. You don't have *popote* in Puerto Rico?"

"Cuca, I never heard of that. It's for arthritis, you say?"

"*Sí, sí,* you soak it in alcohol for two nights, under your bed, and then you make a plaster. Oh it works so good for *artritis*. It goes away. You feel good and you can walk everywhere with no pain."

"No, I never heard of that. But if you find it, let me know where I can get it, and we can have it the store."

"Okay, see you later then." And as she passed San Judas on her way out of the store she said to the statue, "Now you see. You didn't help me today. So you have to help me find *mi popote.*"

But she could not find it anywhere. It truly was becoming a hopeless case.

Cuca returned home just as it was getting dark. As she approached her front steps, she heard someone called her.

"*Doña* Cuca, *Doña* Cuca, it's Ralphie. Can I ask you something?"

"Oh, Ralphie, of course."

"This morning you were asking my mom about *popote.* What is that?"

"Oh it's a *yerba* we have in Mexico for *artritis*. But I can't find it here. Nobody has *popote*. I even prayed to San Judas, but it's hopeless. Even he cannot find it."

"It's a weed right?" asked Ralphie.

"*Sí,sí.*"

"Does it have leaves on it, like five leaves?"

"*Sí,sí,* that sounds like *popote.*"

"Well, I don't want you to tell my mom or dad, but I think I might know where to find it. *Popote*? Right?"

"*Sí,sí*", said Cuca with a sense of excitement.

"But you won't tell my mother or father about this?"

"About *popote*? No, no."

And reaching into his jacket pocket, Ralphie pulled out a small baggie with a few dried crushed leaves in it.

"*Doña* Cuca, is this *popote*?" He proffered her the baggie.

"Oh, Ralphie, you found it. How did you find the *popote*? Nobody has it. San Judas sent you to me." She was grinning from ear to ear. "Ralphie, where can I get a big bag of that? I need to make a plaster."

Ralphie giggled out loud," No, no *Doña* Cuca, you can't just get a big bag of that. It is against the law here. And my parents will kill me if they find out I have even this little bit."

"But Ralphie, why is it against the law? It is for arthritis. It's just a yerba."

"Yea, well, I don't know why. Some people want to make it available for people with cancer, but I don't know. But I'll get killed if I get caught."

"But it's for arthritis, too. Ralphie, you help me get some *popote*. I will pay for it. My knees are killing me every morning."

"Okay, but, our secret, right?"

Ralphie talked to some friends at school.

"You guys will never believe it. My next door neighbor is a lady like about 100 years old and she wants me to buy her pot?"

His friends were incredulous. "Get outta here."

"No, I'm serious. She says it's for her arthritis."

One day *Doña* Cuca stopped Ralphie in front of the house, and quietly slipped him a $50 bill. "Es suficiente? Will that get me a big bag of *popote*?"

"I'll see what I can do", said Ralphie.

Three days later, Ralphie was pacing up and down the block in front of his house like a nervous cat. He was waiting for *Doña* Cuca to show herself. He had been successful and had two bags of *"popote"* stuffed into his jacket pockets. He jumped at every passing car, absolutely paranoid that Chicago's finest had him in their sitès. "Oh, where is that *Doña* Cuca?" he wondered.

"Ts-ts. Ts-ts," Ralphie heard coming from the shadows in the gang way between the houses.

Doña Cuca stepped out of the shadow ever so briefly, and Ralphie ran over to her.

"*Doña* Cuca, I was getting so worried. I could get in so much trouble."

"Did you find *mi popote*, Ralphie?"

"Yea, I have it here."

Looking up Cuca said, "*Ay*, San Judas Tadeo, *gracias*. I so sorry I thought it was hopeless and you send me Ralphie. *Gracias*. I'll light you a candle when I get home."

"*Doña* Cuca, here is your *popote*. And please don't tell my parents. They'll kill me."

"I no tell nobody, Ralphie. But you going to be ok because San Judas is taking care of you. You going to be fine. But I don't tell nobody."

She stuffed the bulging cellophane baggies into her big woven satchel.

When she got home, Cuca laid down her satchel., and took off her coat. She grabbed some matches and a blessed candle from the cabinet and went into her bedroom. She blessed herself with a triple cross: on her forehead, on her lips, over her heart; followed by one more large sign of the cross from head to stomach and from shoulder to shoulder. She placed the candle in front of the statue of San Judas and lit it.

"*Gracias, mi Santito* Judas". "Thank you, my little St. Jude."

She used the diminutive as a sign of respect and special devotion to this saint who had ended what she feared was a lost cause- her search for *popote*. After finishing her homage to the saint, Cuca took four large mason jars from the bottom cabinet in the kitchen. She filled them most of the way with rubbing alcohol and then infused each jar with the *"popote."* As she finished each jar, she blessed it, kissed the cross she had made with her fingers, and placed each under her bed.

For the remainder of March she woke each morning with knees unswollen and ready for her daily walk.

Sometime later, Ralphie ran into *Doña* Cuca out in front again.

"How's the remedy, *Doña* Cuca? He smiled.

"Oh, mi popote is wonderful."

"Doña Cuca, do they have a lot of remedies like that in Mexico?"

"Oh Ralphie, we rarely go to a doctor. God gave us all kinds of yerbas for sickness. Did you go to Mexico with your mother and father?"

"Sure, many times."

"Did you ever get *los chorros*? You know the runny fluid?"

"You mean Montezuma's Revenge? Oh, yeah. My dad too."

'Did you have a remedy?"

"Our cousins got something from the drug store, but it didn't help all that much."

"No, for that you need to drink *te de Yerba Buena.* You drink the tea everyday three times. It tastes so sweet and delicious. Then, when you are better, you drink the same tea and it is terrible, *amarga*, very bitter. That is the sign you are balanced."

"Really?"

"Oh, yes, and if you ever get stung by a scorpion. You must chew three full cloves of fresh *ajo*, garlic. You chew and chew until it is like a *masa*, a pulp. Then you spit that out, and you drink two liters of fresh milk, not from the store."

"And that works?"

"*Sí, sí*. When you get stung you feel the poison here in your throat, slowly choking you. But after you chew the garlic and drink the milk, you lay down, and slowly you will feel your throat open up. You rest one day, and it is gone."

"What? That's wild."

"But, Ralphie, some things make you sick that are not a real illness. But they are poison anyway. This is a spiritual sickness."

Ralphie's eyes widened. *Doña* Cuca always could scare Ralphie with her tales of spirits and other things. One time she told him if he would go to Mexico, and had eyes to see, he could find gold that people hid from Pancho Villa by plastering it in their walls. He loved this stuff.

But *Doña* Cuca turned serious. "Ralphie, you are a nice boy. You are handsome like your father. So you have to be careful someone doesn't put mal de ojo on you."

"*¿Mal de ojo?* You mean evil eye?"

60

"*Sí, sí.* Maybe somebody jealous because you are handsome, or because you are happy. Even if they don't mean to. Do you notice how whenever our people see a pretty baby we always touch the baby, *con una caricia.* If you admire that baby out loud and you don't touch it, you take energy, even life from that baby. You rob it's spirit. Always touch a baby or make a blessing over *la pobre criatura.*"

"Oh, wow, I never heard of that. But, yea, now that you say it, *mi abuela* is always touching people's babies, and me, too."

"She is right, Ralphie." She went on, "You know when I was young in Tepoztlan there was a boy like you. He was from Tejas. A very handsome boy! He came one summer to visit his abuela. But one day, he got sick. He was in bed and was weak. He could hardly move. They called the doctor, and the doctor gave him shots, and they gave him *suero*, you know, sugar water so he would not dry out. But he just got sicker. They even called the priest to come it got so bad. Everybody thought he was going to die. But then the sister of his *abuela* told them to call the *curandera.* They did not want the priest to know, because they do not like *las curanderas.* But she came, *una vieja*, an old lady. She burned some leaves and waved them over the boy. She breathed over him, all over his body. Then she smelled him from head to toe. 'he has the *mal de ojo*' she said. 'Bring me a bowl and bring me an egg fresh from the chicken.' She had the boy turned over and she took the egg and rubbed his body with it. First down his back, then down one arm, then the other, then down one leg and then down the other. She rolled the egg then around his head, and then, whack, she cracked it open and poured the egg into the bowl. And the egg yolk was black!"

"Yikes, then what happened?" asked Ralphie.

Then the old lady just said: 'He will be fine. Make him soup from a chicken for two days. Make him eat it even if doesn't want it. In two days he will be fine. And, Ralphie, in two days the boy was fine. But this was sickness of the spiritual kind. But there are remedies for that, too. But you be careful of the *mal de ojo*. Do you have La Virgen with you?"

Ralphie lifted a medal of the *Virgen de Guadalupe* from under his shirt and showed it to Cuca..

"*Ay, qué bueno.* She will protect you, Ralphie."

"*Doña* Cuca, let me know if you need more *popote*, okay. But remember, please don't tell my mother or father. They'd kill me"

"*Oh no, mi hijo*, they will never kill you. They love you." And with a co-conspirator's smile she added, "But I will never tell them."

The Veneration of the Cross

CHICAGO'S WEATHER WAS IT'S schizophrenic self this second week of April. It had been almost 70 degrees just yesterday. It had turned into a beautiful evening for the traditional Holy Thursday visit to nearby churches. San Silvestre held a mass in three languages last night, four if you count Latin, too.

Alicia Rivera, her husband, Chano, and two of their children took part in the procession from San Silvestre to the other churches. Justo Martínez, the parish deacon, had insisted that the group make sure to stop at St. Hyacinth. "The Polish church always has the most beautiful flowers on the special altar." Alicia conjured the smell of beeswax and incense that wafted through that church last night. She thought how pleasant it was. But her thoughts were interrupted by a cold gust of wind, and a slight mist.

"*Ay*, this Chicago weather is *loco*."

The temperature had dropped almost 30 degrees across the day. Mónica Martínez, the deacon's wife, joined her at the corner, along with several others from the *Círculo de oración*.

"*Ay, tan frio! ¿Cómo están*, ladies? It's another gray cold day in Chicago!" said Alicia. She pulled up her collar some more.

Mónica Martínez, always a very proper Mexican lady, and always a bit more pious than the Puerto Rican ladies, said," *¡Pues, Alicia, es Viernes Santo!* It's Good Friday, and we have to suffer a little bit, *¿qué no?*"

The Puerto Rican ladies laughed when Alicia retorted, "*¡Ay, por Dio, con tanto frio!*"

Mónica repeated, "*Hay que sufrirlo.* We have to endure." And smiled piously again.

Alicia thought to herself, "But I'm a Boricua, and we don't just suffer. *Cuando estoy halto*, when we Puerto Ricans have had enough, well, sometimes you have to fight. But okay, Señor," she added in her interior prayer, "I guess we don't have to complain. And this is your day."

When Alicia got to church, like every Catholic church, the back pews were already filled. And there is no night for church quite like Good Friday night, except maybe Ash Wednesday. So, Alicia had to make her way up to the third pew from the front on the right side section. She rarely sat up here. But as she settled in, she realized it was a great vantage point from which to see who else was in church.

Way back almost to the back pew right on the middle aisle, she saw her *comadre*, Rosa Gonzáles. They had grown up together in Arecibo, Puerto Rico what seemed like a million years ago. They had both come to Chicago when they were eighteen. They had baptized each other's children, and so were more than just good friends. They were *comadres*. Alicia was just bombarded with memories as she spotted Rosa.

In spite of the din typical when this community gathered in church, the choir was rehearsing the Good Friday hymns, and this led Alicia into a kind of reverie. That was when the memories started pouring forth. Then she saw in her mind the face of her *comadre* and best friend, Rosa, again.

Alicia's memory went back to that day last June when she missed the bus out in front of Gonzáles' Food and Liquors. She always seemed to miss that bus. She ducked into the store knowing Rosa and Tito would both be working there. Rosa sat behind the check out counter as she entered.

"Ay, comadre, me perdió la wawa, again."

Rosa came from behind the counter and the two women embraced. Alicia was her usual hyper self, but quickly noted that Rosa was not herself. She and Rosa had this intuitive aspect of their relationship that had been that thing that always let them talk to each other about anything and everything. They just figured the other already knew anyway.

"Nena, what's the matter? You don't look yourself. Is something going on?"

"I'm pregnant", Rosa said softly, almost timidly.

"Oh, how wonderful, comai! When did you find out? Ay, you didn't call me. And I didn't even guess!"

But Rosa smiled sadly, shrugged, and put her head down. Alicia saw the tears welling in Rosa's eyes.

"What's the matter, m'ija?"

"Tito is not so happy about this."

"'But why? What's the matter with him?'"

"He says he's too old," Rosa said, clearly repeating something that she did not understand.

"Rosa, you are NOT too old! I know for some women it's get dangerous if they are, but you are not too old!"

"No, no, Alicia, he says he is too old."

"¿*Qué*? Did Tito get stupid or something?"

"I know", Rosa said finally letting her sadness give way to let her exasperation show.

They talked some more. And then, Alicia asked with a humph," Where is that *Viejo sucio*?"

"Oh, out in the back room,"

And Alicia remembered how out she went to the back room to see poor Tito. She had to smile and she thought again about Monica Martínez and the Mexican ladies and how unlike the Puerto Rican ladies they were. Alicia once said to Rosa, "The Mexican ladies get all quiet when their men go *machista* on them. But you know, not us Portorras. Our men run when they piss us off."

"*Compai*", shouted Alicia as she went into the back storeroom. "I hear you are going to have a baby. *Ay, papi chulo,* you old devil. You still got fire in the furnace, eh?"

Tito was conflicted. He loved the seductive compliment to his manhood, but his unhappiness with the situation got the best of him. And he just frowned back at Alicia.

"*Ay. compai*, how can you make Rosa feel like that? She's supposed to be happy and you are making her sad. What's the matter with you?"

"Ma Alicia, I am too old." Tito bleated.

"Too old? What are you talking about? It's Rosa who has to worry about being too old. And she is fine."

"I know, I know, she's fine. But what is going to happen if that baby is a boy and then he grows up. When he is a teenager I will be over seventy, and he won't obey me or respect me. He'll talk back to me. And I won't be a man anymore."

"Oh por Dio, you men are so stupid sometimes! What are you thinking? You're a grown man and afraid of baby, macho stupido. That baby is from God and you better not insult God. You go tell Rosa you love her and that baby!"

This was not simply a recommendation. Alicia stood her ground, until Tito went out to the storefront toward Rosa.

"Mama Alicia, the bus is coming. Ya viene la wawa." shouted Rosa.

Alicia had flown out the door that day almost missing the bus again.

Alicia's remembering was interrupted. A drum beat sounded through the church, rhythmic, slow, instilling a sense of silent tension among the congregation. Six men, all in black, stiff and silent carried a life size wooden cross from the back of the church toward the altar. Fr. Figueroa, Deacon Martínez and other ministers followed. Three times the group stopped and Deacon Martínez sang out loudly, "*Mirad el árbol de la cruz;*

67

behold the tree of the cross on which hung the Savior of the world."

Reaching the front of the church the men laid the wooden cross almost vertically against the steps going up to the altar. Then came the ministers, who all prostrated themselves on the floor in silence. All was silent, dramatic, except for a few fidgeting infants.

The ministers rose and went to their chairs. The service followed including a long reading of the Passion of the Christ. And then Fr. Figueroa began to speak,

"We stand here before a scene of death. Our people are no strangers to death. We all face death and sadness in our lives. How many of you sitting here tonight have been touched by these things? Our neighborhood faces death and sadness. There is death and sadness in many of the countries from which we have come. But did you see this wooden cross as the men carried it in? It makes one thing so clear: Jesus himself faced sadness too, and he faced death and it took him. He even screamed out: '*Dios mío, Dios mío,* why have you abandoned me?'

Alicia heard no more of his sermon. "Why have you abandoned me?" The words echoed in her mind. "*Ay, my poor comadre.! Poor Rosa,*" she thought, "*God abandoned her.*"

And her thoughts turned back to that terrible day when Rosa's world seemed to have collapsed. When to Alicia it seemed that God had abandoned her friend.

Her memories of that day in February were vivid. It was gray, cold and damp. Alicia made a point to visit Rosa every day now as her due date was closing in. Rosa had insisted on working every morning at the store as long as she could. Alicia was convinced this was to minimize Tito's aggravation with the whole pregnancy. *"Tan salvaje son los hombres! Men are savages,"* she thought, and then blessed herself for thinking so badly about such an old friend in such a holy place.

That black day Rosa was seated behind the counter as usual when Alicia got there. Rosa told her she had opened the store at 7:00 and made the big urn of coffee for "los Milleniums" as called them, the young rich *americanos* moving more frequently into the neighborhood.

"They aren't like the old neighborhood people. They just come in, fix their coffee, and hold out money. No hello, no thank you. They don't even look at you in the eye, only at their phones. *Comadre*, I feel so sorry for them."

"I know, *comai*, they have good jobs, and fancy cars, but they are so unfriendly," added Alicia.

"Well, I think they must have a lot of pressure," said Rosa trying to understand her new customers.

"But they seem so *maleducados*, Rosa. They don't know how to talk to people. Sometimes I think they don't even see us. I wonder how their parents brought them up." Alicia had far less sympathy for these neighborhood newcomers.

"Well, at least they are good for business, Alicia. They come every day now for coffee in the morning, and they like to buy the wine and beer especially for Thursday and Friday. That makes Tito happy. So we got to change and accept them." Rosa concluded with that shy smile of hers.

And then suddenly, she whined in pain, "*Ay* Alicia, he's kicking again." Alicia was around the counter in a flash. Rosa almost whispered, "I think the water broke."

"*Ay Dio mío*, Rosa, we have to go to the hospital. Where is Tito?"

"Ooh," Rosa groaned again. "He is coming later. Call him at home, Alicia."

Alicia dialed and Rosa's teenage daughter, Doris, answered. "Dori, this is Ma Alicia. *El bebé ya viene.* Your mommy's baby is coming now. Where is *tu papi*?"

Doris' voice cracked as she answered, "He left a long time ago for the store. He should be there by now. Is *mami* okay?"

"*Sí, nena*, but she needs to go to the hospital now. Tell your papi. I will get her there we can't wait. Tell him meet us there. Can somebody come to the store?"

"I will come now and I will call my cousin, Edwin. He knows how to run the store."

"Okay, *nena*. I am going to take *mami* now."

Alicia ran out in front of the store to see if she could catch a cab, but spotted her Mexican neighbor, Poncho Velasco, parking down the block.

"Poncho," Alicia shouted.

"Hola, Alicia. ¿Cómo estás?"

"Poncho, there is an emergency. Rosa's baby is coming. Please help us to get to the hospital."

Poncho ran back to the car and pulled it up in front of Gonzáles' Food and Liquors. Alicia was already helping Rosa to the car.

She spotted Doris and Edwin about a block away, and yelled, "I am taking *mami* now. Tell your *papi* to come to the hospital when he gets here."

And off they sped to the old Norwegian Hospital a half mile away. At the hospital Rosa was immediately taken up to delivery. Alicia waited for Tito to arrive. She was stunned when she saw Doris and Edwin frantically come through the lobby and running toward the emergency room.

"¿*Dori, qué pasa*? Where's your *papi*?"

"On my God, Ma Alicia, something is the matter with him. We found him in the back store room. He was there all the time when you and *mami* were there. They think he had a stroke or something." Poor Doris was shaking and crying.

"Dori, your *mami* is upstairs having the baby."

"And my *papi* is back there," she said pointing to the emergency room. "He wasn't moving when we found him, Ma Alicia. He was making this weird noise."

"Okay, *nena*. It's going to be okay."

Alicia remembered though; it wasn't okay. While Rosa was upstairs giving birth to a little boy, she remembered, Tito, who was so threatened by the birth of a son to a man too old, was breathing his last. "*Ay, mi pobre comai*, "she thought, "*en un solo día, her life was un revolu. Turned upside down. And poor Tito, mi compai.*"

The music brought Alicia's attention back to the Good Friday Service.

"Perdona tu pueblo, Señor. Perdona tu pueblo. Perdónalo, Señor", the sad Good Friday hymn interrupted Alicia's thought.

Fr. Figueroa was standing in front of the assembly holding up that large wooden cross with help from the other ministers, and people were already inching forward in no particular order. It was just a sea of people, moving slowly, silently. The ushers trying to bring some semblance of order were simply overwhelmed.

Alicia bowed and kissed the wood. *"Señor Jesucristo, ayúdanos,"* She blessed herself as she prayed.

She made it back to her pew and from there watched the throng moving forward silently. She recognized many but again found the face of her *comadre*, Rosa, in the midst of the crowd coming up the center aisle. She could not quite make out baby Robertito in Rosa's arms.

"Ay," thought Alicia," Mi *comadre* must feel like Jesus, abandonada por Dios."

And Alicia remembered the days and weeks following that happy and black day. Alicia remembered Rosa sitting in a wheel chair holding the baby as she was brought into the church for Tito's funeral. The baby was named Robertito. Rosa insisted he be named for his father. One day he would also be called Tito.

Alicia remembered the nine nights, the *novenario* of rosaries, for Tito that followed. She remembered visiting Rosa at home early in the day of that ninth night. Alicia again saw a deep sadness in Rosa's face.

"*Comai,* you look so sad today. I know you miss him so much."

"I do miss Tito, *comai.* But it's not that. I heard from the doctor a little while ago." She began to sob. "I don't know what to do any more. My poor baby!"

"But he is such a beautiful baby, Rosa!" said Alicia.

"Yes, he is beautiful. I love him so much. But the doctor told me he has some problems, Alicia. They think he is a Downes baby. You know, he might have problems as he grows up."

"*My poor comai,*" thought Alicia as she was jarred back into the Good Friday Service.

It was time for communion and the people next to her wanted to get out and go up to receive it. She moved her legs so they could pass. She just couldn't bring herself to go up there today.

Alicia watched as people took communion from the priests, they paused and bowed to the wooden cross. But she found herself feeling the full weight of the abandonment it represented.

Then she remembered the words of Madre Tecla at the women's retreat last year. She told them about one of the great saints, Santa Teresa, a Latina like them. Sister Tecla told the ladies, "*Teresa was a mujer determinada con una gran determinación.* A determined woman, with a great determination."

"Ladies," the nun told them," One time St. Teresa was feeling very sad and abandoned. She prayed and prayed and prayed, and nothing. She felt nothing. So, she changed her prayer. She said, 'Oh Senor, they say you are the one true friend, but if this is how you treat your friends, no wonder you have so few of them." Alicia thought the Mexican ladies were a bit scandalized by this. But she and Rosa and the other Puerto Rican ladies roared laughing and all said afterwards they thought St. Teresa must have been a *Puertorriqueña*."

Alicia saw Rosa holding Robertito with one hand out to receive the wafer from the priest. She thought her friend looked serene somehow.

"*¿Pero cómo?*" Alicia asked herself. "How can she do it?"

Alicia surprised herself at how bitter she felt toward God at that moment. She remembered, "*As if Rosa's life wasn't already un revolu, how could you send those tax men to her? On top of everything else?*" She was asking God directly and accusingly.

About a month previous Rosa had a visit from an agent of the IRS and the Illinois Department of Revenue. They were looking for the tax payments, and liquor revenue payments that Tito had not sent for more than a year and a half. The amount totaled into the tens of thousands of dollars.

"How could you let such a thing happen to Rosa?" was all the prayer that Alicia could muster at that moment.

Again Good Friday intruded on her thoughts. The drum began to beat that slow rhythmic toll. And with that a core of women clad in black came forward to the wooden cross. The oldest ladies began to wrap the cross in ribbons of white and gold. The younger women then came forward each carrying bunches of flower: mums, roses, gladioli. They kept coming, more and more, and piling the flowers all around the wooden cross and then on top of it.

The choir began a hymn beloved in Puerto Rico.

"*Santa María de la esperanza, manten el ritmo de nuestra espera, manten el ritmo de nuestra espera*". "Holy Mary of our Hope, maintain the rythm, maintain the rhythm of our hoping."

And then a woman with a deep and powerful voice chanted the verses. Alicia was just filled with emotion at hearing this voice, these words. Nostalgia, sorrow, grief, shame, even a flash of anger. When the third verse came, the words penetrated to her core. "You lived with the cross of hope, holding your love in a deeper hope…Holy María, maintain the rythm of our hope, maintain the rhythm of our hope."

As the service concluded it was as though no one wanted to leave, but all were invited to come forward one last time. There were baskets of flowers: carnations and daisies. Each was invited to pray and toss a flower onto the growing tribute to the cross. Some people even placed photos onto the pile. One young couple placed a teddy bear

Rosa still holding Robertito was waiting with her daughter Doris, her nephew Edwin, and other friends out in front of church. It was still cold and crisp.

"Alicia, come over to the house. I'll make a nice Bustelo. *¿Hace frío, no?*" said Rosa.

"Ok," responded Alicia," but let me run home first. *Tengo un pi de manzana*, a nice apple pie, and I'll bring it over."

It felt so good to get inside out of the cold night. And the aroma of the Bustelo filled the whole house. Rosa had invited a few neighbors over. The men, as usual, sat in the living room, and the women gravitated to the kitchen.

"*¿Ay, tan linda fue la misa, no?*" asked Frances López, Rosa's Mexican neighbor.

The ladies all began to speak animatedly about the service, and then quickly got into the latest neighborhood gossip. Alicia thought as she looked around the room, "*Puro bochinche, pure gossip.*" Then she remembered bochinche was a Puerto Rican word. The Mexican ladies just called it "*comadriando*", just being *comadres*. This thought made Alicia laugh, "Just being *comadres*."

Alicia stayed after the other guests had all left, after all she was *comadre* to Rosa, and that was her right. "Just being *comadres*", Alicia thought again with a smile, but she had an urgent question for Rosa, and one she had to wait for the others to leave so she could ask it.

"Rosa, it was so beautiful in church tonight but it made me think a lot. And what the priest said, and the music. *Ay Dio mío*, I was *conmovida*."

"I felt so at peace tonight, Alicia", said Rosa.

"I know, *comai*. I could see you walking with the baby to kiss the cross, and to go to take communion. And I kept thinking how God abandoned Jesus, and Jesus was crying out to him. And I kept thinking, *Dio me perdone*, that God abandoned you these past few months. Don't you feel that way sometimes?"

"*Pues*, Ma Alicia, I just felt so sad some days. It seemed like every day was something else. I still don't know what I can do about the store. There's so many taxes. I am probably going to have to sell it. I don't know. But, you know with all that I never really felt like God abandoned me." She got quiet for a moment. "Alicia, I'll tell you the trut all I could think was thank God I had Him. I lost my husband. My baby has so many problems. I am probably going to lose the store. How am I going to make money and feed my children? But every day I feel God close to me, like a best friend. God felt closer to me than ever."

"Rosa, when I heard the song to la Virgen, Santa María de la Esperanza., I remembered when we were still girls in Arecibo. You remember how they sang that song in our church. It always made me cry. I cried tonight in church too. I am glad you are feeling peace. Maybe I was the one who thought God abandoned you; maybe all of us. Then the lady sang those words, 'You lived with the cross of hope, con la cruz de esperanza.'"

"Alicia, I think we have to hope like that. I wouldn't make it through one day if I didn't. I ask La Visne to give me strength to take whatever cross the Lord gives me."

"*Así se venera la cruz*, right? That's how we venerate the cross, no?"

Rosa smiled her timid smile and said in the tone of a Pentecostal preacher, "Amen, Hallelujah!"

And the two *comadres* broke into laughter.

Something Beautiful

"CAN I HELP YOU FIND something beautiful?"

Chris Mahon was taken aback by the question. It seemed an odd turn of phrase, and he wasn't sure it was directed to him.

But he quickly heard again, "Can I help you find something beautiful?"

Looking up Chris saw the sales clerk looking directly at him.

"Oh, my God," thought Chris to himself, "I have just found something beautiful."

The sales clerk was indeed an incredibly handsome Latin man. Chris was so stunned he was at a loss for words, which rarely happened. Before he could recover his inner composure, the sales clerk smiled a broad grin. His smooth brown skin contrasted his pearly white teeth. His brown eyes seemed to dance. He seemed to know that his beauty had caught Chris off guard. He only smiled more broadly, seeming to enjoy the moment, and completely comfortable in his skin.

Then he added, "We have so many beautiful things here. I am sure you will find something you love."

"My God, he is adorable," thought Chris. "He could sell me the Brooklyn Bridge." But Chris recovered, and said, "Yes, I am looking for a gift for my mother for Mother's Day."

"Oh, for your mother! That is so nice. Let me show you these beautiful things we have here."

Chris thought he picked up a hint of an accent. He found himself just mesmerized by this young man.

The sales clerk asked, "Does your mother love Lladró? This is such beautiful porcelain. Over here let me show you we have these beautiful little boxes from France."

He showed Chris a selection of Limoges boxes. Their colorful cloisonné was indeed lovely.

"I love to work here. I am surrounded by all these beautiful things all day. I feel so lucky."

"Have you worked here for a while?," Chris asked desperate to start a conversation and to know who this man was.

"Oh no, I have just been here three weeks. I was visiting some of my family in Miami. One of their friends invited me to come to Chicago and I fell in love with this city. It is so beautiful. I saw the architecture, and then the Lake Michigan. Such beautiful buildings. And everybody is so nice. And the night life is so much fun."

This last line was accompanied by that wide playful grin again, and a slight knowing raise of the eyebrow.

"My God,", Chris thought, "unless my gaydar is off, he's gay and he thinks I'm gay."

But the sales clerk went on without pausing, "So I decided to stay here. And a guy I met at a club that first day told me I should come here to work at Bloomingdale's." He shrugged his shoulders and smiled, "I can't believe how lucky I am. And now I get to work surrounded by all these beautiful things."

Completely intrigued, Chris asked, "Where are you from originally?"

"Well, I come from Nicaragua originally."

"But you speak English with almost no accent."

"Thanks. I studied English in my country when I was little. I wanted to go to art school but my family had to leave because of the Sandinistas. We went to Houston for a few years. I guess I grew up there. All the rest of my family went to Miami. But, you know," he said wistfully, "Houston is kinda boring. So I went to visit my family in Miami. Now...here I am in Chicago." Smiling again, he said, "And I love it here. So I am going to stay here."

"*¿Cómo te llamas?* What is your name?" Chris finally asked.

"Nicanor is my name. Nicanor Castillo. My friends call me Nico, though. You speak Spanish?"

"Well, yes, at least enough *para defenderme*, as they say."

"No, your Spanish is beautiful, too. How did you learn it? And what is your name?"

"Nico, my name is Chris. Chris Mahon. It is so nice to meet you." Nico shot that wide grin again. "And I learned

Spanish a few years ago. It's a long story, but I went to Mexico a few summers ago to learn Spanish."

"Excuse me," interrupted another customer, "may I see the Steuben glass vase in the case over there?"

"Oh yes, ma'am. That is very beautiful. I am happy to show it to you" said Nicanor warmly.

Turning to Chris, Nico said, "Look around, and I'll be right back. Okay, Chris. And then we'll find something beautiful for your mother."

Chris' eyes followed Nico across the floor as he went to attend the woman looking for the Steuben glass. *"My God, he is an angel,"* thought Chris. Then, *"Oh, Christopher, be careful; don't get your hopes too high on this one. What would this guy ever see in you!"*

But within minutes Nico was back. Chris had decided on a Lladró angel. The angel seemed to be blowing a good night kiss.

"This is so beautiful," said Nico. "Let me get it wrapped up for you. They have beautiful paper for Mother's Day, too."

While Chris waited he was aware that he did not want this shopping excursion to end. He had never felt quite like this before. He was usually in control. But he thought, *"My heart will break if I don't get to see this man again."*

Nicanor came from a back room with the wrapped package in his hands. The wrapping was indeed beautiful!

"Here you go, Chris. Your mother is going to love this."

"I know she will, Nico. She'll even love the wrapping paper. Thank you so much for your help on this," Chris hesitated.

"Are going from downtown now?" Nico asked.

"No. I would browse around some more as long as I'm here."

'Well I get a break in about fifteen minutes. I want to invite you for a coffee."

Again that broad grin and that mischievous raising of his eyebrow.

"That would be wonderful!"

Chris could not contain his enthusiasm.

"Okay, I will meet you at the Starbucks across the street on Wabash."

Nico put Chris' package in a big bag with handles.

Chris wanted to kiss him right then and there, but controlled himself.

Quickly but carefully, he rushed out of the store and across the street to Starbucks. He didn't want to chance missing Nico's arrival, and he wanted to secure one of the quiet corners.

When Nico arrived he waved at Chris and without asking Chris he went straight away and ordered them each a cappuccino grande.

"Here you go, Chris." Again Nico was grinning that broad smile. "I am so happy you said you would have coffee. I have to be honest I wanted to see you again."

Chris was bowled over. Never in his experience had he met somebody who seemed so comfortable in his skin. Certainly none of his "American" friends seemed so sexual, and so comfortable with their sexuality.

Chris mustered up the courage, actually more easily than he would have thought now that he was sitting across from Nico, to say, "Nico, I wanted to be with you again, too. But I wasn't sure how to make that happen."

"That's because you are shy. I like that about you already. So, do you have a boyfriend? Or maybe you have a girlfriend?"

"No, Nico, no boyfriend. And I wouldn't worry about a girlfriend."

"That's what I thought. Well, maybe that's what I hoped." Nico got very quiet for a moment. Still smiling, his eyes became much more intense, "You know you are a very handsome man. And I love those touches of gray hair you have on the sides. But your eyes…they are so beautiful. You have beautiful blue eyes."

Chris was blushing incredibly. He could feel the heat in his cheeks. Nico saw this and smiled again,

"Look I made you red. You are so sweet."

"Nico," Chris almost giggled it out," I thought you were an angel when I first saw you."

Nico seemed to get a kick out of that and added, "But maybe I am a little devil, too." They both locked eyes, smiling at each other.

"Nico, do you think we could have coffee again sometime?"

"How about when we wake up tomorrow morning?" Nico said laughing. "Well, I gotta get back to work now."

And as he got up he handed Chris a note. Then he got up to go back to work, he leaned over and kissed Chris on the cheek, right there, in the middle of Starbucks. Chris was practically giddy.

When he opened the note he found Nico's name and phone number and a small message: "You are beautiful. I hope you call me soon."

When Chris got home he found himself nervously passing the note from one hand to another. Was he crazy? Should he forget this ever happened? What did he know about this guy? Would his friends widen their circle to let him in? Did Nico feel about him the way Chris was imagining, hoping? Finally, he couldn't help himself. He had to make sure he was not in some dream. He had to make sure Nico was not one of those handsome angels from the bible who shows up from time to time, and then vanishes.

It was almost 9:00 p.m. Nico had to be back from work by now. Chris dialed. It rang…and rang…and rang. But there was no answer.

"*Oh God, what a fool I am,*" Chris thought. "*He is probably out at one of the clubs moving on to his next conquest.*"

But at 10:00 p.m. Chris' doorbell rang. He lived in a 3rd floor walk-up. And so he had to use the intercom to find out who was there.

"Who is it?"

The voice was soft, almost subdued, and thus almost not recognizable.

"Is this Chris? This is Nico."

"Who? Nico? Nico, is that you? Just a minute. I'll come down."

"How did Nico get my address? Who is he with? Is this okay or is this something weird going on here?" All these things went through his head when he went down the stairs.

Chris could not believe his eyes. There was Nico. Alone. Grinning still but with what looked like tears in his eyes.

"Nico, come in, come in. But how did you get my address? I realized when I got home this afternoon I had yours but I never gave you my contacts."

"Oh, don't get me in trouble, but I just looked at the sales credit slip again so I could find you."

Without waiting he dropped the bag he was carrying and hugged Chris. "I just wanted to be with you. My friends are nice. But I had to see you."

They entered the apartment and without any more words they were kissing and wriggling out of their clothes.

In the morning, as Nico had hoped, they had coffee again. But they went back to bed and made love again.

Laying there side by side Chris commented, "Look how white I am and how brown you are."

Nico said, "It's like cappuccino." Then, more thoughtfully, he added, "Chris, in art class we call this chiaroscuro, the play of light and dark. It makes a nice picture, don't you think?"

"Yes, it does, Nico. It surely does." And then, "Nico, will you stay?"

"Yes, Chris, if you want me to."

"I do, I do." Nico began to laugh. "Hey, that's sounds like we're getting married."

Mother's Day came and Chris' mother did indeed lover her angel. Chris loved his. The days following were the happiest Chris could ever remember.

Chris spoke to Emma Schmidt, the old German landlady, to make sure she was okay with having another young man around. Emma for her part was delighted. She had lived in this three flat building since she first came from Germany as little girl over 80 years ago. The neighborhood was all German, Bohemian, and Polish in those days. Then, it had become Puerto Rican and Mexican for about twenty years. But now it was changing again. It was gentrifying. The good news for Emma was that the rents on the 2nd and 3rd floor apartments were going up. The challenge for Emma was that the taxes were soaring, too. And the cost of maintenance, even just getting the garbage downstairs, or the sidewalk shoveled when it snowed was getting out of sight. Emma was crafty, however. She once told Gertrude Claus, one of the other older German holdouts down the block, that she always wanted to rent to young men. But she would keep their rent low, and she would let them know just how low she kept the rent for them. In exchange, the young men never seemed to mind when she asked them to take down the trash or shovel the walk.

Chris brought Nico down to meet Emma a few days later.

"Oh come in, come in. I am glad to meet you. Sit down, boys. Do you want some coffee? I just made some strudel."

Sharing the coffee and strudel. Emma said," Now boys, we'll keep the rent the same. I am just so happy Chris, you have such a nice friend."

Chris and Nico looked at each other and smiled.

Catching that look, Emma went on, "I like the boys that are moving into the neighborhood. You know, Nico, I lived in this very building for more than 80 years. Some years it was not so good to walk around here. We old ladies never would go to anything even at Church at night. But you boys are making things nice. We old timers feel safe again. "

Chris added, "the neighborhood is changing, Emma, isn't it? But it is so nice to see the diversity here. I hope it doesn't get urbanized."

"Oh, there were so many changes. You know that nice Mrs. Arroyo sold her store. Now it is Starbucks, But you know when I was little, it was Geoppinger's butcher shop. Then I think it was Steinhauser's hardware store. But I like the nice boys moving in."

Chris thought, *"It is at the edge of "Boys Town."*

But sooner or later it would revert to wealthy professional families.

Nico was telling Emma about coming from Nicaragua, and his love for art and beautiful things. Emma was showing him some old photographs and two oil paintings in the living room. And then there he saw the Steuben glass bowl. Nico's eye lit up.

Emma asked, "Do you know this glass?"

"Oh yes, We sell Steuben glass at the store. It is so beautiful. Someday I want to open an art studio downtown. I want to fill it with beautiful things like this bowl. I think people should be around beautiful things like this. It just makes people feel better, and even be better."

This exchange touched Emma. Her mother often said something similar. When Emma and Mary were little, their mother would also have them listen to music on the old fashioned Victrola. She thought if people could hear beautiful music, they would become better people.

"Nico, we gotta go." Christ interrupted. "Thanks, Emma for everything."

"Oh yes, Emma, thank you. The strudel was delicious."

As he got up to go Nico added, "Emma, I love to paint, so if you ever need anything to be painted, I will be happy to do it." Emma smiled with delight.

After a week or so, Nico asked, "Chris, something we never talked about is on my mind."

"What?"

"Do you go to Church? I am a Catholic, you know, and I like to go to Church"

"Nico, I'm a Catholic, too. But…well, I kind of stopped going. I go when I am with my family. But not around here so much."

"But I like to go to Church. I love it there. I feel so good there. You know when I was little in Nicaragua my "*abuela*" would take me. And she would show me the saints, and the beautiful paintings. Up on the ceiling there beautiful angels, and the Mother of God. We always felt safe and surrounded by beauty. You know our country was pretty crazy in those days. It meant a lot. How come you don't like to go?"

"Nico, my family is Irish. That means we are a pretty Catholic, too. Remember when I told you I went to study Spanish in Mexico? Well, I was in the seminary."

"You wanted to be a priest? Oh, my God."

"I thought I did. And I wanted to work with Spanish-speaking people. That's why I went to study in Mexico. But it was when I was in Mexico that I starting getting in touch with my real feelings, when I could admit I was gay. When I got back to the seminary I had to wrestle with that. Well, I felt the Church doesn't exactly like gay people. I was sure I would have been a good priest, but I had to admit I was also gay."

Nico listened intently. "So what happened," he asked.

"Well, I guess my Irish guilt kicked in. I got confused. I found myself getting angry at the Church. There I was all ready to become a priest, but I was also gay and wanted to accept that in me. I wanted to be celibate, and I wanted to love another man. Nothing was making sense anymore. My folks knew I was unhappy, but I didn't think they could ever understand why. This issue was not something we would ever really talk about. But my dad one night just said, 'Son, being a priest isn't for everybody. If you were ever going to be unhappy in that life, you shouldn't force it. Your mom and I want you to know we support you whatever you decide to do.' So at the end of that year I left the seminary."

"Did you go looking for a boyfriend?" asked Nico.

"No, not really. I just felt guilty and pretty angry. Any time I got close, I pulled back. I went with friends to the bars. But it was like I was always the designated driver. I was just the window shopper. When I moved in here, I just never bothered to make any connection to the church. Although, I think Emma has probably done a few novenas for me."

"But, why do you say the Church doesn't like gay people?" Nico seemed puzzled. "Everybody is a sinner, and we' re supposed to go there and get rid of our sins and feel good again." He went on, "Chris, I have always been gay, and I am Catholic, and I love the Church, and Jesus loves me. Did somebody tell you Jesus didn't love you?"

"Well, no, not really. It just felt, I don't know, not comfortable anymore."

"But that is in your heart, Chris. You gotta be the one to take that out. Nobody can tell you Jesus doesn't love you, because they are big sinners, too. Jesus told me he loves me. That made me happy. So I go to Church to be happy."

Chris was mulling all this. "So you want to go to Church?"

"Yes, I would like to go to Church. But I would like you to go with me, too."

"We'll see," Chris said, but he already knew he would go with Nico.

The following Sunday morning Chris told Nico they had three choices of churches they could walk to: a small, growing young adult church. St. Tecla; St. Eulalia, which was also a Catholic center for the nearby university; or Saint Sylvester, mostly called San Silvestre now. This church had a very diverse congregation of old Germans, like Emma Schmidt; Puerto Ricans and Mexicans, and a growing number of gay couples from nearby Boys Town. They opted for Saint Sylvester.

Nico fell in love with the church the minute he saw it. It was in the German Gothic style, with high stained glass windows. Inside they found frescoes at each of the fourteen stations.

"It is so beautiful!" Nico exclaimed. "I want to come to this church."

Although Chris was fluent in Spanish, and Nico would have been even more comfortable attending mass in that language, Chris insisted they go to the 10:30 mass in English. His friends told him there was a fine choir for that mass. He also thought there would not be children running all over the place like at the noon Spanish mass.

The choir was rather extraordinary. Nico was just in some rapture, with the music, and the quite fine art work.

He whispered to Chris," It's beautiful here."

When the lector began to do the first reading, Nico sat up with that grin of his. Chris, too, noticed a distinct sibilance, almost a hiss with each letter "s." Chris thought to himself, *"My God, it's the hiss that could shatter glass!"*

But it was Nico who nudged him, and whispered, "And you think the church doesn't like gay people?"

When communion came both Chris and Nico noticed what to them appeared to be several gay couples going forward. Chris then noticed the lesbians who owned the local book store on their way up with their children. He was surprised to see them there.

"Nico, those are the lesbians from the book store."

"And you think the church doesn't like gay people?"

Chris was confused, but when he turned to look at Nico, he saw him smiling serenely. The confusion fell away. He loved this man even more than he could have ever imagined.

When it came to their aisle to go forward to communion, Nico sat down. Chris asked, "Aren't you coming?"

"No, Chris, I am a sinner, first I need to confess. So I have to wait."

The other people in the pew were getting impatient so Chris stepped out and went forward.

After mass Chris asked: "Why didn't you go? I felt like a goof standing there."

"But Chris, were you happy to go and take communion?"

"Well, I guess so."

"I was so happy to see you go up there. Next time, when I confess, I will go up there with you." And then that wide grin of his," I told you the church loves gay people. Jesus loves gay people. He loves us."

"And I love you, you idiot."

All at once Chris felt he had his faith back. This wonderful man loved him. Jesus Himself loved him.

"Nico, you are something-something beautiful!"

Tres Pelos

HERMELINDA CARRASCO FELT that the clothes were still a bit damp and so put six more quarters in the slot to start the drying cycle over again.

"*Ay*, these dryers never dry the clothes on one cycle. I think they set them this way to get more money."

This was her weekly lament at *La Lavandería* Suds-O-Matic.

"Someday I'm gonna have my washer and dryer right in my own house. Then, no more of this lugging this bag over here and waiting forever for the clothes to get dry."

Sonia López just chuckled. She and Hermelinda followed this same ritual every week. They lived across the street from each other. Every Saturday they each lugged two big bags of laundry down their apartment building steps, met out in front and struggled to stuff the bags into collapsible wired carts with wheels for the two block walk down the street to the Laundromat. They always went early to avoid the crowd. But the dryers always seemed to take forever to drive, and, of course, six more quarters.

In reality, however, both Sonia and Hermelinda looked forward to this time together to catch up with each other. After putting the laundry into the washing machines Hermelinda would go two doors down to the Supermercado El Timón to get two cups of Mexican coffee, and a bag of *buñuelos*, sugary little pastries. This was part of the Saturday ritual, too. Upon returning to the Laundromat, Sonia and Hermelinda got down to what they both called the hour for *comadriando*, a little catching up, a little gossip, and often enough a lot of laughter.

"So, Sonia, I have to tell you what happen yesterday at work. You know that manayer I always talk about, the one I call *Tres Pelos*, you remember I told you he is the one with three hairs, and he comb them over this way?"

She made a sweeping, combing gesture, to suggest tossing the three hairs from the part on the right side of his head to the far left. Sonia burst out laughing, and Hermelinda giggled and went on.

"Well you know like this," repeating the gesture. At that the two women broke out laughing.

"*Sí, sí, comadre*", giggled Sonia.

"But, I have to tell you, Sonia, they are three long hairs." And she made that combing gesture again. The two women convulsed with laughter.

"But no, Sonia, that guy made me so mad yesterday. You know I told you I was already mad at him from before when he was playing with our schedules just to upset us. That time I called the union, and they got him to behave. But we were all mad at him and the hotel already when they change the number of rooms they want us to clean every day."

Sonia got serious, too. "Hermelinda, I still don't understand how they can get away with telling you to clean more rooms, but you don't get any more money, and you have to do it in the same amount of time as before. You know we came to America to get away from people like that."

"I know, Sonia. You're right, from eight rooms a day, now we have to do sixteen. They say if the people don't check out, we can do a light dusting of the room. And now they put out a card for the guests to sign that says they don't even want clean towels or sheets. Huh, that is a joke. You should see how some of these people leave the rooms. They are *cochinos*, real pigs. And you have to clean up extra. But even when the guests are clean and nice people, we don't want to do just a light dusting. They are gonna be unhappy with us, and we are proud of our work. We want them to see we do a good job and not think bad about our people."

"Sometimes over here they treat us like we are just peones on some big hacienda. It's like they never heard of Benito Juarez. Or Pancho Villa", added Sonia smiling.

"Sonia, you are so right about that. Benito Juarez had the best advice: *el respeto de los derechos ajenos es la paz.* I remember that from *la primaria.* Sometimes at my hotel we know they don't respect us. It shows in so many ways. It's like we are a bunch of burros."

"Hermelinda, last week I ran into Gladys DeLeón, and her sister, Chabela. They work at a hotel, too, but it sounds like a bad one. And they don't have a union like you do. Nobody can stand up for them. They told me they had a bad manayer, like the one you have. He is some *gringo*, but maybe not born here, but from Polonia or some other *gringo* country. Well, he decided to make a poster with the picture of all the housekeepers on it. But just their faces. Then, he took their face and attach it to a *caricatura*, you know, like a cartoon body. But all the ladies' bodies were in bikini, and you know like *cuchi, cuchi*." Sonia wiggled her breasts like a go-go dancer.

Hermelinda gasped. *"Ay, sinvergüenzas"*.

"Oh, Gladys told me she was so mad when she saw this. She told me Chabela just starting crying when she saw her face on the vavoom body."

Sonia wiggled her breasts again. "But Gladys told me Chabela cried out loud: '¡Me tratan como una puta! ' Then, Gladys told me she got so mad she went and ripped all the caricaturas down and tore them up. She told me, 'Chabela is right. They are treating us like whores!' But then the manayer came and he screamed at Gladys. He told her and Chabela to go to his office immediately. Gladys said they were scared, and when they went to his office he screamed at them again and told them they were fired."

Hermelinda was horrified at the story. "You see Sonia. These manayers think they can get away with *disrespeto* like that. I even heard from some housekeepers that they try to get them alone in the room, while they are cleaning. Of course, we have some guests who try that stuff, too. But believe me, I don't care what hotel, that stuff goes on."

Sonia asked: "Hermelinda, is it true all the housekeepers are gonna get a boton now? You know a button to push if somebody get fresh with you?"

"*Sí, sí*", said Hermelinda. "Our union got the city council to make a law and the hotel have to protect us now. We call it HOPO. That means you better keep your hands off, and you pants on. That's why I am so lucky in my hotel we are a union. We're gonna get those buttons, and we got a contract, and it includes they have to respect us. But let me tell you about Tres Pelos yesterday. I swear that man is so stupid. And I told you one of these days he was going to tangle with me and I was going to fix him at his own game." Hermelinda's face changed from a serious frown to a half smile and a determined look.

"So, I just finished cleaning my first eight rooms at the hotel. I had six rooms for guests staying, you know, the light dusting." Hermelinda rolled her eyes. "I also had two check outs which, you know, requires much more work. *Gracias a Dios*, these guest were not *cochinos*. They didn't leave *un desmadre*. But there I was on my knees scrubbing those bathroom floors, reaching to the top of the dressers to dust. You know I am pretty *chaparrita*, so I have to get a chair to reach. Sonia, can you believe that manayer will not agree to get us those dusters with the longer handles so we can reach better without hurting our shoulder. Huh, Tres Pelos doesn't care about us. I told you sometimes they treat us like *burros*.

So Sonia, I just finished flipping my eighth jumbo mattress. *Ay Dios*, my shoulder and my elbow were killing me so I took my break. Oh yea, Tres Pelos," Hermelinda made that sweeping combing gesture again and both women started laughing again, "doesn't want us to get our breaks either. Sometimes he stands out in the hall telling us to hurry to the next room. But my union told him it is my right to have a fifteen minute break. So anyway, I went to the lunch room to take my break, whether Tres Pelos likes it or not. You know I carry my union contract with me all the time- in English and Spanish, just in case he wants to give me any trouble. I know he doesn't like me, but too bad for him. But, ooh, I got him good yesterday." Hermelinda could not hide her sense of satisfaction.

"*Dime*," said Sonia. "Tell me what happened?"

"Well when I went down to the lunchroom for my break. I saw this new worker. Her name is Marilú Jiménez. She is one of the newest housekeepers. I started to say hi, but I saw she looked very flustered, and upset. I could see she was crying. So I said to her, '*M'ija*, what's the matter? Are you okay? *¿Qué pasa, m'hija?*'

"She told me that a manayer yelled at her for speaking Spanish. She was so scared. You could see her shaking. She said that manayer told her he would write her up if he caught her doing that again."

"Sonia, you know this is so typical of these guys. They are just insecure men who just want to show who is the boss. But I swear to you, Sonia, I am not going to take this from anybody, even if it was just an insecure woman who was the boss. This is *disrespeto puro*. It got me pissed off like my union lady says."

"So, I said to Marilú, '*M'ija*, you stop that crying right now." And I pulled out the contract from my pocket. 'Do you have a copy of our union contract? Did you ever read it?' And I shook that contract at Marilu. 'Don't you sit there crying. You stop that right now. You have a contract. You go home tonight and you read this because you have rights. And nobody can disrespect you in this hotel.'"

"I gave her my copy and told her I wanted to see her tomorrow and she better tell me she read the whole thing. Then I asked her,' Okay, *M'ija*, now I wanna know which manayer talked to you this way?' "

"Marilú got quiet. I knew she was scared. 'I wanna know which manayer made you cry like this? Don't you be afraid, you gotta contract. Look right here on page seventeen, in the paragraph', and I showed her,' it says any worker can use their native language. You see it is in the contract. The manayer broke the contract. You tell me which one it was. It wasn't the one who looks like he has tres pelos combed over his head, was it?'

Hermelinda couldn't help making the combing gesture again, and giggling a bit in the re-telling of the incident.

'*Pues, sí,*' said Marilú, 'it was that one'

"I went like that again, making that combing. So it was Tres Pelos, was it?'

"*Sí,*" said Marilu. "That is the one."

"Well you go home and read your contract, I'll go see him. He broke the contract. He is in big trouble."

"Sonia, you know me. I was so mad at that Tres Pelos, but I knew I had him. So I went to the H.R. office and stuck my head in and there he was. 'Excuse me, I need to speak with you briefly.' 'Sure, come in, Hermelinda,' he said to me. 'What can I do for you?' He asked me, looking at his watch.

That pissed me off, too. I thought of my union lady again.

"Well, I asked him, do you read?"

"'Of course, I read', he answered very rude to me."

"Which language do you read? English or Spanish?" And I could tell he was getting annoyed, but I didn't care. "Which one?"

"English."

"Okay, good. Will you read this paragraph here on page seventeen?"

"What?"

"Can you just read me this part right here?" And I showed him again where on the page.

"*Every employee has the right to use his or her own language while at the work place.*"

"Okay, stop. That is the part. And that contract is signed by your bosses with the union, right?"

He just nodded back to me, but I knew he was confused, and I think, a little scared of me at that moment.

"So why did you break the contract your bosses signed?"

"What do you mean?" he asks.

And, boy, he was paying attention to me now.

"I mean you broke the contract your bosses signed with the union. You told the new housekeeper, Marilú, you would fire her if you caught her speaking Spanish here again. You broke the contract."

"Well, I…"

He was very flustered, but like I learned from the union,

"I was there to give the message so I did not let him interrupt me. 'You broke the contract and I am going to have to write you up and report you to the union.'"

"Sonia, I loved to tell him I would write him up. That is Tres Pelos' favorite line when he wants to bully us housekeepers."

"He was so scared now, Sonia," Hermelinda reported triumphantly. "He was like a *tartamudo*, you know, Sonia, 'well, but I, but, well, uh, uh, uh. So I said to him, 'Okay, this is what we are going to do. First you are going to go to Marilú and apologize to her. And you tell her she can e-speak e-Spanish whenever she wants to in this hotel. You scared her and made her cry. When she tells me you apologized to her, then we can forget the incident. If you don't apologize today, I will write you up and call the union, and they will call your bosses, and your bosses will ask you why you broke their word.'

He said, 'oh, this is such a misunderstanding.'

I put my hand up and said, 'This is no misunderstanding. You broke the contract. Go and apologize or I write you up. You know, you want to have peace with all of us. I believe that about you. In my country one of our great heroes, Benito Juárez, said: "*El respeto de los derechos ajenos es la paz*". Let me put it in English: respect for the rights of others is peace. *Señor,* respect goes along way. But in case it doesn't, we have this contract.'

'Yes, I understand,' he said, 'I will go apologize right now.'

"Sonia, I couldn't believe it. Tres Pelos got up right then and there and he apologized to Marilú."

"Hermelinda, you may have to be careful about Tres Pelos when you go back to work. You have to be careful with little men like that. He will try to trap you."

"Sonia, if he wants peace in that place, he better not tangle with me or with my union. First he better respect me, and all of us housekeepers. If he doesn't, we have a contract, and his bosses gave their word. I think it is even the law. I think maybe a good contract is stronger than Tres Pelos, or any little men like him. You know even Papa Francisco said that the future of humanity doesn't belong to the powerful and the elite people but us people and in our ability to organize. I saw him on Univision the other night and he was saying that. And now we got Papa Francisco on our side, too. And that's why we organize a union- because of guys like Tres Pelos."

The *Tocayo*

THE RECTORY PHONE RANG just after 10:00 a.m. It was a hot, humid July day. It was also a Monday, and Father Jim Ryan was tired from a full weekend of masses, weddings, and baptisms. He had had half an idea to grab a good book and a blanket and drive over to the beach this morning. He had just slipped out of his black priest clothes and into a tee shirt and a pair of shorts. He could already feel the cool Lake Michigan water on his legs. He was about to call one of his other newly ordained classmates to see if he was free this morning, but before he could dial the house intercom's harsh buzz interrupted him.

"Oh God, not today, please," he said to himself as he picked up the phone.

"Father, Esther Rodríguez is on the phone. She sounds kind of upset, too," said Mildred Henkes, the parish secretary.

"Thanks, Mildred. I guess I better talk to her," said Ryan, conscious that his tone was a slight bit sarcastic. He could see Mildred in his mind, picking up on that, nodding her head, and rolling her eyes in agreement, and enjoying the irony in his voice.

Esther Rodríguez was the parish busy body, and Mildred had cued him into that fact a week after his arrival two months ago. Mildred had been the parish secretary for thirty-one years. She knew everyone. She was very professional with the parishioners and very loyal to the priests. Some thought of her as rather too protective of the priests, which if true, Ryan was beginning to appreciate very much. In any case, Mildred was one of those people who could communicate a good deal with very few words. When she said Esther Rodríguez was on the phone and seemed kind of upset, Mildred was letting Ryan know that she had tried to screen this call any number of ways but without success.

While the intercom buzzer had unnerved Ryan already, that was nothing compared to the dread he felt knowing Esther Rodríguez was on the other end of the phone. In these two short months Ryan had already had multiple encounters with Esther. She tended to button hole him either in the sacristy just before mass, or on the church steps as he finished mass. Her purpose was inevitably to report on someone's transgressions in church, or to try to get Ryan to show up at one event or another that she had a hand in.

Esther Rodríguez, more formally Maria Esther Reyes de Rodríguez, had come from Guanajuato, Mexico with her sister and two brothers. The four of them settled in Chicago. She later married a Tejano named Manny Rodríguez. Because she was, through her husband, and now the births of her four children, a green card holder on her way to becoming a citizen, she held a certain position among the other women in the barrio. She was something of a *comadre* to everyone, although no one had ever asked her to stand as godmother to their children. She kept tabs on everyone, and everyone's kids. And, as Ryan, had picked up from Mildred and the other priests, Esther could be something of a nuisance to the priests, too often encouraging them to intervene in various troubled domestic situations, in which she had been the original instigation.

"Watch out for that woman," the retired monsignor had warned Ryan the first time her name came up at the dinner table.

Quickly Ryan had his own first hand experience of Esther trying to impose her way about something. Upon hearing that he might take on responsibility for the Teen Club, she wanted him to impose a certain program the parish staff had rejected earlier. All of sudden Ryan was getting calls from parents, and visits from a few well -rehearsed teen agers asking for the program. Ryan was only ordained a few weeks and was still hoping to avoid any major conflicts in his first year in ministry. Still he found Esther's style troubling. He did not like her passive, yet aggressive manner.

Fr. Casey, his pastor, suggested, "Jim, you may be encountering what we call '*la indirecta.*' You'll have to get used to that working in the Mexican community. Someone in the community wants or needs to get something done, but, for some reason, rather than going directly at it, like we *Gringo*s might, they come at you sideways. Somebody else you didn't expect becomes the spokesman. Maybe to us it feels manipulative... but it's just another culture, and another way of getting things done."

"You just finished studying Spanish, didn't you? Did you ever use the passive subjunctive in English? Well, you'll hear a lot of the passive subjunctive here, and a lot of "*Si, Dios quiere*", if God wills it," chimed in the retired monsignor. "I found that usually means: 'I know what you are asking, but I won't be able to fulfill your request."

"The *indirecta* is a way of saying no," added Fr. Casey. "I think it may be more the Indian influence on the Mexican culture. You don't find this so much in the Puerto Rican community."

The conversation led Ryan to reflect on his own Irish culture for a moment, and what he supposed to some could be the annoying way his parents and aunts and uncles tended to answer a question with another question. The Irish certainly had their "*indirectas.*" And although he immediately felt guilty for it, Ryan still thought of Esther as manipulative and passive-aggressive.

Ryan braced himself as reached for the phone. He said to himself, "*You are a new priest. Don't let her get you going. No matter what, be nice.*"

And then into the phone he said, "Hello, this is Fr. Ryan."

"*Buenos días, Padre*", Esther began.

Ryan was sure her tone communicated, "Well, I've got you this time. You'll have to do what I ask today."

But Ryan was wrong, and Mildred had been right. There was something different in Esther's tone this morning. And nothing indirect. Her voice was urgent.

"*Padre*, a boy is dying, They live across the street from us in the big apartment building."

She referred to the run-down six flat building that dominated the corner at 24th Street and Kildare.

"The family, *Padre*, they don't go to church, but their boy is dying. Please you have to come. Yesterday they went to look for a priest at the rectory but no one was home. Please, *Padre*, you will go to them, no?"

Ryan sensed her urgency, but he also felt a resistance welling up inside of himself. It was hot. It was Monday morning. He was tired enough already. He had never been with a dying person. He realized this was the true source of his resistance. His thoughts were panicked. The prospect of meeting death chilled him. He was frozen in a moment of internal conflict. "*I am a new priest. I cannot deny the dying the sacraments. And for a child, for Christ's sake! But Esther is a meddler and is probably exaggerating the situation.*" Ryan struck a compromise with himself.

"Esther, this sounds very serious, but maybe these people don't want a priest. You said they don't go to church. They might not want me just butting in."

"But, *Padre*, they went looking for a priest yesterday and they couldn't find one. A little while ago the man came to my door and asked me to get a priest for them because they know I go to church."

"Esther, I would like to make sure. Will you have the people call me?"

"*Ay, Padre,*" Esther sighed with exasperation as she hung up the phone.

Ryan hoped that would be the end of it, but he was left feeling guilty and unsettled. *"God, how could you be so cowardly!"* he recriminated with himself. *"If a boy is dying you need to be there. This is why you became a priest."*

Still in yet another moment of self-assertion, he hoped to salvage his day at the beach; or at least minimally to avoid this unfolding encounter.

The intercom buzzed rudely again fifteen minutes later. It was Mildred again, "Father, there's a lady on the phone, but she only speaks Spanish. I can't get what she says. I can hardly hear her she is so soft, but she asked for the *padre*. Do you want to take this call?"

Swallowing his dread, Jim Ryan said, "Yes, Mildred. I will take this call." And he thought to himself, *"Well, Esther, I guess you were telling the truth. Here goes."* And again into the phone he greeted her, *"Buenos días."*

"Ay, padre," the woman began softly. *"Mi nombre es Ema Nellie Sánchez, Padre.* I am the neighbor of María Esther, *Padre.* She said I should call you and you would come, *Padre.* Will you come, Padre?"

There was no mention of the boy, so Ryan took the initiative. "You want me to come and anoint your son, I understand. Is his situation grave?" Ryan could hear himself, and thought, "How clinical can you get! This lady needs some compassion here."

"Sí, Padre, está muy mal. He is very bad. Will you come, *Padre*? We went for you yesterday, *Padre,* but we couldn't find

anyone. But today, *Padre*, I think this is his day. He needs the blessing to get over, *Padre*."

"I am on my way," said Ryan and hung up.

Ryan dressed quickly back into his clerical clothes. He grabbed the Spanish language ritual book with the prayers for the dying and the oil stock with holy oils. He ran the two blocks to the old apartment building, prodded on by genuine concern, and a good dose of guilt for his earlier reluctance. His fear, however, was only just slightly out of his awareness.

Coming to the apartment building he couldn't immediately find the front entrance. He walked along the side of the building and came to the back stairs. He paused for a moment unsure of where to go, when he heard a shout from the third floor porch.

"*Padre*, we are up here," said a young man in his early twenties.

Ryan bounded up the three flights of stairs to where the young man was standing. "I am Ray, *Padre*."

"Ray, I am Fr. Ryan, I mean, well, everybody calls me *Padre* Jaime."

Ray gave Ryan a puzzled expression for a second, "Come in, *Padre* Jaime."

And then he opened the back door to the third floor walk-up and ushered Ryan into the kitchen of the flat. As they entered a woman was standing in the kitchen. She had dark brown skin, but what struck Ryan were her very blue eyes and a long braid draped over one shoulder. She looked very anxious and had been crying.

"Ma, this is *Padre* Jaime," Ray introduced her to the priest.

Her look was of complete puzzlement and shock. But she never took her eyes off the priest. Softly, she asked," You, you are *Padre* Jaime?"

"*Sí, sí,* soy *Padre* Jaime," Ryan answered both puzzled and concerned at the way the woman kept staring at him.

"And what is your name?" he asked the woman.

"I am Ema Nellie, *Padre.* This is my son Ramón. Enrique, my husband, is in there with my baby, *Padre.*"

Ryan looked past her into the living room and saw an older man seated next to a bed. He saw someone was resting on the bed.

When he returned his gaze to the kitchen, Ema Nellie was still staring at the priest. She asked again, but very softly, "Your name it is Jaime?"

The woman's expression changed from one of anxiety to amazement, and finally, if Ryan was reading her accurately, to joy. "Jaime?" she questioned again.

Ryan nodded, and then added, "Well in English, it is James. But in Spanish, *sí,* it is Jaime." Ryan thought Ema Nellie's face seemed to fill with a look of joy and wonder. This only unsettled Ryan all the more.

Ema Nellie's eyes well with tears as she breathed out his name very softly, "Jaime."

Suddenly she shouted in to the man in the living room, "Enrique, *mira*, Enrique, *ha llegado su tocayo*. Our son's *tocayo* has come. *Y es un sacerdote*. He is a priest."

Enrique stroked his dying son's head and stood up to look at the priest who was now standing in the living room doorway.

"*¡Bendito sea Dios!*" he said, and made the sign of the cross over himself, and then over his son lying on the bed in the living room.

Ema Nellie turned to her older son, Ray, "Ramón, it will be today for our baby, *hijo*. *Padre* Jaime has come. He is your brother's *tocayo*, and he is a priest. He will help him across today. *Es su día*. This is his day."

Ryan was now utterly mystified. His fear of meeting death face to face was still at work, but his mind was baffled by this mysterious talk of a *tocayo*.

"*Padre* Jaime, please come in," Enrique said tearfully as he beckoned Ryan into the living room.

For a brief moment Enrique seemed consoled that God would not betray or abandon his helpless son. His approach to the priest was almost supplicant. He seemed almost a desperate man eager to please one who held the power of life and death over him. Enrique was a hurting man, playing an uncommon role for him, but not uncommon to men whose hearts are broken and at the edge of despair. He reached out his hand to greet Fr. Ryan and Ryan noticed the dirty cracked fingers as he stretched out to shake his hand. "*A laborer, a mechanic,*" thought Ryan. This is a tough man in a man's world, but helpless and humiliated by the cancer killing his son.

"I am Enrique, *Padre*, and this is my son…"

Enrique began to sob. Ryan put his hand on the man's shoulder but said nothing.

Ema Nellie stepped forward and took Enrique's hand. Then she knelt and reached out to the teenage boy laying on the bed, and stroking his hair she said, "*Jaimito, Jaimito, mira, hijo, tu tocayo ha llegado. Padre Jaimito* is here for you. Jaime your *tocayo* has come."

That was the moment Ryan remembered the significance of the *tocayo*. Two people with the same name share a spiritual bond and with the saint whose name they carry. Ryan's deep Celtic sensitivity moved him to let out that small gasp of recognition the Irish use when they are overwhelmed by mystery.

Ray, the older brother, had hung back in the kitchen, but Ema Nellie beckoned him to come to the side of the bed.

"Ramón, *Padre* will say the prayers now, *mi hijo.*"

Ray knelt alongside of the bed, but apart from his mother and father. He was silent and looked empty, an older brother robbed of the opportunity to mentor and resent.

Ryan got busy with the ritual book and the holy oils. He drew the family close around the bed.

"*En el nombre del Padre...,*" Ryan began. "By this holy anointing may the Lord in His love and mercy help you with the grace of the Holy Spirit. May the Lord who frees you from sin save you and raise you."

Even as he said these words, however, the boy's breathing took on and odd rattling sound. He seemed to gasp two or three times on every inhale. The exhale was one long, rattling sigh. "*Padre* nuestro..."

Ryan continued the prayers. But in his head he was trying to keep out his growing panic, and awareness that this boy was dying.

Ryan finished the ritual and sat with the family in silence. "*What do I do now? Good pastoral practice says I can't just rush out of here.*" But panic was the real issue for him. "*How do I get out of here?*" he wondered.

And, then, certainly out of his nervousness he asked out loud to Ema Nellie and Enrique, "Do you want to call the doctor now, or maybe the ambulance?"

No one seemed to hear his question. Each family member was holding on to little Jaime. But finally Ema Nellie said, "No, *Padre*. They would just come and take Jaimito from us, and he would die alone and afraid someplace. We brought him home here, *Padre*, where he feels safe. We don't want him to die with strangers. Here we can be with him to help him. And now you are here, *Padre*. You are our son's *tocayo*. You have the same name, the same protector saint, and you have spiritual power. You are a priest. You are the one to help our Jaime to cross *para el más allá*."

The reality came crashing in on Ryan: what he had feared most in this whole incident was now directly in front of him. He was to see the face of death. In the silence, the rattling breath seemed to get louder. In the silence, Ryan's own heart beat loudly, wanting to flee, and yet wanting to serve as a true priest in this poor moment of human misery.

The intervals between the inhaling gasps and the exhaling sighs got shorter and fainter. Mother, father, and brother each placed a hand on little Jaime. Then, slowly, Jim Ryan reached out his hand, too, and placed it on the boy's arm. Then there was no more struggle, no more gasping, just one last breath and then stillness.

Later Ryan would swear he saw a shadow cover the boy and watched as his complexion became blue-gray under the shadow. The shadow then passed, and Jaimito in one long, low rattle, exhaled his spirit. He had crossed to the other side.

Ryan reflected to himself, "*I might have been this boy's tocayo and helped him across to the other side. But surely he was my tocayo and helped me to face death. We will always be linked together now.*"

Enrique spoke first, "*¡Es como una aurora!* It is like a sunrise for our son." He stroked his dead son's hair as he spoke. "*Padre* Jaime, our son was always weak. He was born with problems. He had epilepsy. Then he got cancer and lost his leg. He has always needed our help. But now he is free."

Ema Nellie now took her turn to grieve her lost son. She held the body of her son across her lap like a Mexican Pieta.

Ray sat in brooding silence with, it seemed, no one to console him.

After a long period of silence, Enrique turned to Ryan and asked, "*Padre*, what do we do now?"

"We need to call the undertaker, Enrique."

"But we don't know anybody, *Padre*."

"Enrique, I will call the local undertaker here. He is a good man and people here trust him very much. I will call him." Ryan finally felt useful and back in some measure of control of circumstances.

He called the Burek Funeral Home around the corner. "Norm, this is Fr. Ryan. I am with a family and their son has just died at home. Norm, they need our help. They really have nothing, and they are just at a loss about what to do."

"Father, don't worry about a thing. We will take care of them. What is the address? We'll be there within the hour."

Some days after Jaime's funeral, Ema Nellie came to see Fr. Ryan.

"*Padre* Jaime, I had a dream, and I saw *mi* Jaimito. *Ay*, *Padre* Jaime, he called to me. I saw him and he was naked like he always was running around as a little boy. But, *Padre* Jaime, he was a grown man and he had both of his legs. And he was not retarded, *Padre* Jaime. He jumped and laughed and showed me he could even dance. Then, *Padre* Jaime, he sat in a giant chair. There were many chairs. And *mi hijo* told me they were the chairs of Jesus and the *Santos Apóstoles*. But *mi Jaimito* was

116

playing on the chairs and sitting naked. *Ha llegado, Padre* Jaime. My son arrived. I wanted you to know he crossed over to *el más allá, Padre* Jaime."

"Ema Nellie, tell me about Jaime, about *mi tocayo*. I want to know more about him," said Ryan.

"Ay, *Padre* Jaime, it was not easy for Jaimito ever. First he was a surprise for me and Enrique, and Enrique was not happy to have a baby. Then we found out he did not have enough oxygen when he was born. We noticed right away that he was handicapped and he was mentally different. Enrique felt this was *un castigo de Dios*, and he blamed me. One night he got very drunk and accused me that Jaimito was not his son, but from somebody else. But, *Padre* Jaime, Jaimito was his son. But we both blamed God. We were miserable. Oh, *Padre*, we were not very good *católicos. Mi* Ramón never made his communion. We never went to church and we never took Jaimito there. But, *Padre* Jaime, we told him about *La Virgen*, and about Jesus, and he always loved when we made *la bendición* over him. He would smile so happy."

Ema Nellie went on, "*Padre* Jaime, Jaimito made us laugh. He was simple. He was always a baby. He was sixteen when he died, but he was always like a baby. He was *un inocente*. But in his life he always needed help to sit up, to eat, to go peepee, for everything. We did our best, *Padre* Jaime. But thank God, you came that day, because he needed help again and we could not get him across ourselves. Thank God He sent you, our baby's *tocayo*. And I know he is happy where he is. Gracias, *Padre* Jaime."

Ryan had to admit the entire incident had shaken him to his roots and yet he was strangely consoled by it at the same time. For Christmas later that year friends gave him an icon of St. James, his patron saint. As he set it up on his book shelf, Ryan found himself speaking to the saint, "Well, I hope you like this spot. You can keep an eye on things from here. After all, you are mi *tocayo*."

August: *"Así Es La Vida"*

CHICAGO WAS SWELTERING ONCE AGAIN as the "dog days" of August set in. In the neighborhood gang violence interrupted life daily with tragic results. Seven young men had been murdered so far this month: shot, stabbed, and, in one incredibly gruesome incident, skinned alive. Just yesterday a five year old girl was killed by a bullet from a passing car as she sat on her front steps. Last week a two year old toddler strayed into the path of a car being pursued by another. The young mother froze in her tracks as she watched the death of her baby unfold before her eyes in slow motion. Neither car stopped.

Ray Ruiz mulled over each of these tragedies. He had been personally drawn into each of them. He was the local undertaker. For Ray there was a name attached to each tragedy, and real families left reeling with horror and loss. And Ray tried to do his best for each one.

Ray was pensive this morning, He had seen a lot already in the fourteen years since he took over the funeral home from Chester Simec. Old Mr. Simec had built up a good business over the years serving the Bohemian immigrants who built the neighborhood. Ray wondered aloud, "I wonder if Mr. Simec ever had a summer quite like this?"

Ray remembered he first met Mr. Simec when as a young boy his family moved from Laredo, Texas into the house next door to the Simec's. Mr. Simec and his wife had always taken an interest in Ray and when he was in high school they hired him to answer the phones in the funeral parlor in the evenings. In those days, Ray remembered, wakes were pretty routine affairs, mostly of elderly folks who had passed away after long illnesses or just old age. The old Bohemian wakes were also pretty quiet affairs.

"Boy, they were stoic people," Ray thought. "But those were my kind of wakes," he said to himself.

Ray chuckled as he thought of his wife Lety telling him just last night, "Ray, sometimes I think you are an Old Bohemian, the way you act. Are you sure you are Latino?"

"Lety," he retorted, "you gotta admit our Latino wakes are dramatic. And you never know if someone is going to get hysterical, or carry-on, or if a fight will break out. I prefer the old Bohemian wakes. No drama. You know how things are going to go."

"You know, Lety," he had added, "I never thought this business would be like this So many young people. It's supposed to be mostly old people, but we get so many kids. I mean, I suppose on the one hand I shouldn't complain: we got a lot of business. But, sometimes, all these kids, it just gets to me. I wish we weren't burying so many kids."

Ray remembered how Lety had just nestled into him last night as she said, "I know, *mi amor*, it's been tough. But we'll get through it. Next week kids go back to school, and the weather will get cooler soon, and this craziness will stop for a while."

In the morning Lety was up ahead of Ray. He could smell the strong Mexican coffee all the way upstairs. He enjoyed the slight scent of cinnamon Lety always put in the coffee.

"Where are the girls?" Ray asked.

"Honey, they already had breakfast. They are next door with Marilú. Marilú was Lety's cousin, who had two daughters almost the same ages as her and Ray's two girls.

As Ray started his breakfast his mind was already at the funeral parlor. He reflected that all the skills old Mr. Simec had taught him were coming into play these days. The worst situation he could remember Mr. Simec having to deal with was an elderly couple who had died in a house fire. The bodies were burned pretty badly. And Ray remembered the grieving and somewhat guilt-ridden and alienated family they had to deal with at the wake.

Lety sat down with a cup of coffee, and Ray said, "Lety, you know, the worst Mr. Simec ever had to deal with was that elderly couple that were burned in the house fire. I think for us, it was that teenager last summer."

"You mean that kid that was electrocuted on the El tracks?"

"Yea, They called him Rabbit. Rudy López, Jr. was his name, though. That was so sad."

"But how did he get up on the El tracks at 3:00 in the morning?"

"You know these kids. He and his friends were drinking and smoking and he got the crazy idea to spray paint rabbit ears up on the signs along the El tracks. He slipped, hit that third rail, and zap." Ray seemed to be reliving the whole horrible event.

"*Amor, por favor*," Lety said. "You're getting morbid."

"Sorry, Sweetie." Ray was quiet for a moment and then added, "You know, Lety, sometimes I don't understand our people. I mean, Lety, I am Mexican, too, but I don't get the way people act. It wasn't like that when we lived in Texas. It wasn't that way in this neighborhood when the Bohemians were here. I mean, I was here with them, too. But we didn't have all this craziness." Ray was getting emotional as he spoke, "And some of these funerals, I mean, Lety, you have to admit, they get emotional. You know last week I couldn't get people to leave the cemetery. And those gangbanger funerals...O my God! They are different. After all the prayers, these guys have their rituals. They even pour tequila into the grave. What the hell is that all about? I was so glad the *padre* had already left to go back to church."

"Ramón, *amor*," Lety kissed Ray's ear in a gesture to calm him.

"Well, it's true, Lety." She hugged him and nibbled his ear a little more. And it was having its effect.

"Ramón, you expect everyone to be like those old Bohemians. But people are different. Your people are from Texas, and they do things differently. My people are from Mexico, and that sure is different from Texas. You know,

Ramón, *mi abuelo* had an expression he used whenever things happened he didn't fully understand, or when he didn't seem to have any control over them. He would shrug his shoulders and say, '*Así es la vida*'. When something was strange to him, he didn't judge it. If people acted different than folks back in our village, he just used that phrase: "*Así es la vida*".

Lety nibbled on Ray's ear a little more. "*Que nos seas tan gringuito, mi amor*...don't be such a *gringo*, my love. You should be like my *abuelo*. Don't let these things get to you. ¡*Así es la vida*!"

Ray swung around in his chair and nestled his head into Lety's stomach, and began to nibble on her. He grinned up at her and then began to stand slowly. He took Lety into his arms and just uttered a guttural "Grrrr."

"Hey, Lety, I am just a man," he said with a mischievous look. "¿*Así es la vida, no?*"

Lety broke up laughing and pushed him away playfully, "Ay. *Cochino*, you're a dirty old man."

They did love each other.

As Ray started the door Lety shouted after him, "Ramón, remember tonight is Chabela's birthday. I told Jorge we would be over at 7:00 p.m. Chabela still doesn't know he's making a party for her."

Ray was fond of his *compadres*, Chabela and Jorge. And it brightened his mood considerably thinking of getting together with them tonight. They had known them for several years. Chabela was from the same town where Lety was from in Mexico. When she and Jorge had first come from Mexico they lived around the corner from Ray and Lety. They were a natural choice for Lety and Ray to invite to be godparents for the second daughter, and in some ways and more importantly, to become *compadres* to each other. Chabela was probably Lety's best friend, and Ray thought Jorge had to be one of the funniest people he had ever met, although he had to admit his Spanish was not so good that he caught all of Jorge's punch lines.

Chabela and Jorge had been married eight years and as yet had no children. Ray had once made a comment about this to Lety, but she had only put her index finger to his lips, and said nothing. He knew enough not to bring that subject up again. He just assumed there was some problem in conceiving children and felt sorry for them. But the subject was left unspoken. Chabela and Jorge had tried for over four years to conceive a child. What Ray did not know, but what Chabela had shared with Lety, was that doctors had pretty much ruled out children for them.

But Ray returned to the happy thoughts of the evening ahead with his *compadres*. But again that phrase popped into Ray's mind, "*Así es la vida*".

In fact, the phrase kept popping into Ray's mind all morning. About 11:00 a.m. Father Alex stuck his head in the front door of the funeral parlor to say hello.

"Anybody home?" the father shouted.

"I am in here in the office, *Padre*, come on in. You want some coffee?"

"Great. I was taking communion around to some of the neighbors here. I thought I would just say hello."

Ray noticed the priest looked a bit weary, or maybe troubled. They had been spending a lot of time together lately because of the rash of gang related deaths. They enjoyed each other's company. Ray put the coffee down in front of the priest.

"*Padre*, it's been pretty tough lately around here. How are you holding up?"

"Ray, I gotta admit, it shakes up my faith. Getting a handle on it is tough. I keep asking myself; 'how do we break this cycle? What can we do? What is God's plan in all of this?'

It didn't surprise Ray that even the parish priest would have his faith shaken by this summer's events. Father Alex and Ray were a lot alike. Like Ray, Father Alex was Mexican-American, but born here in Chicago.

"You know, Ray, sometimes I don't understand our people. Where does all this violence come from?"

The words stung Ray for a moment. "*Padre*, I know exactly what you are saying. Lety and I were talking about this this morning. I don't understand our people either. Lety tells me I think too much like a *gringo*, or that I act like the old Bohemians. Just this morning she told me to be more like her *abuelo*, and when things didn't make a lot of sense, he just shrugged and said, "*Así es la vida*".

"You know, Ray, maybe she is right. The old time Mexicans do say that a lot. To me it always sounds passive or even submissive, and I want to take things on and change them. But that often just leaves me feeling angry. The old timers went

125

through a lot of tough times. Maybe that '*Así es la vida*' attitude got them through them."

"Well, I'm like you. I want us to take control of the situation. All this gang stuff, all these kids dying, I want to do something, not just give up and shrug and say: '*Así es la vida*'."

"Ray, I always believed preaching the gospel was a way of saying to people: things don't have to be this way. There is an alternative. I bristle a bit when I hear this passive *así es la vida* thing. But, I am beginning to think there may be a wisdom in it. Anyway, Ray, one of the reasons I wanted to stop by was to let you know I think we are going to have another really sad one coming in."

"What's up, *padre*?" Ray was all alert.

"You know the Villaseñor family over on 27th Street, don't you?"

"Are they the ones with about five kids?" Ray asked visualizing Tony Villaseñor with a flock of kids around him.

"Yea, Ray, they have five kids, and another one on the way, actually due almost any day now. But Margarita, the wife, has had a real hard time during this pregnancy. She has passed out a few times, and more recently she could not keep her balance. Ray, they found out last week she has an inoperable brain tumor. They hope she will have the baby before it gets worse, but she seems to be going downhill fast."

The priest paused to take a sip of his coffee.

Ray just sat silent, feeling genuine sadness. "That poor woman", he said, and added, "that poor man with all those kids. What is he going to do? A man can't manage a big family like that without a woman."

Ray and the priest sat in silence for a long time.

"Well, Ray, I better be getting back to the parish. Thanks for the coffee." He smiled, and as he was about to slip out the door he stuck his head back in and added, "Keep the Faith, Ray."

"You, too, *Padre*."

Ray sat contemplating this piece of news, but he did not have long to wait for the call requesting him to begin to make the arrangements for Margarita Villaseñor. The punch to Ray's gut came though when the caller added the words "and her new baby." Ray was dumb struck. "But we don't lose mothers and babies in child birth any more. How can this be?"

Margarita Villaseñor had slipped away far more quickly than anyone had imagined, taking her unborn child with her.

It was about 1:00 p.m. when Tony Villaseñor, accompanied by his *compadre*, Miguel de Leon, and his brother Carlos, and his oldest son, Junior, came to the funeral home. As they entered, Ray was standing in the front hall way. Not a word passed between them. Ray just opened his arms and embraced Tony, with no words, the only sound being that made by Ray's hands as he patted Tony's back. Ray then invited the men and the boy into his office. Ray walked through his check list and to each item Tony Villaseñor looked at Ray, then at his *compadre*, who would nod, and then back at Ray nodding his assent. Ray knew finances would be difficult for this family so he guided the mourners to the least costly items: a cloth covered wood coffin, a single pillow, two stands of flowers. Ray had assumed that this body would be shipped back to Mexico as were so many in this neighborhood.

But Tony Villaseñor was firm: "No, it will be here. My kids is here now. How could they see their mother in *Méjico*?"

Ray suggested a grave at St. Mary's cemetery. It was the cemetery of choice lately among the Mexicans, and Ray knew he could secure a Catholic Charities grave, and the cement vault for less than $600.

To all of this Tony Villaseñor nodded his assent.

Then, Miguel de Leon spoke to Tony, "*Compadre*, we have to talk about the baby, too."

Ray anticipated this and jumped in with an offer, "We can get a small coffin for the baby. It will be like his mother's."

Tony began to cry. All the other men bit their lips or stared at their shoes. There is nothing else for other men to do when a strong stoic man like Tony breaks in their company.

Then Tony said, "No, I don't want the little *criatura* to be away from his mommy. He's too small, and he will be too lonely. I want you to put him in with his mommy. She gonna hold him to God."

As the men and the boy left, Ray felt completely drained, but strangely satisfied that he had served these folks well. He held the image of Tony Villaseñor and his oldest son in his mind for a time and then said to himself, "*That poor man; that poor, poor man*" And then oddly, he found himself wondering how such things happen, and more oddly sighing and saying, *"Así es la vida"*.

It was almost four o'clock by the time Ray was able stop and pick up the body of Margarita Villaseñor and her baby. Ray had asked Andy Luczak and Eddie López, who were buddies of his from mortuary school, and who also had small parlors not too far away if they could help him with the embalming. They were at the funeral home when Ray got back from the hospital morgue.

At 6:30 Lety called, *"Amor*, you didn't forget about Chabela's party did you?"

"No, no, Sweetie, I'll be right there."

Ray could not convey how eager he was to get out of the funeral home and to be together with Chabela and Jorge.

Jorge had sent Chabela and her sister out on some errand so that they would not return until 8:00 p.m. He knew that no party ever really began until everybody was there. And he knew he would never get everybody there by 8:00 p.m. unless he told them to be there by 7:00 p.m. He was right, and by 7:30 all the principles were on hand.

When Chabela came in the door a few minutes after 8;00 p.m. she jumped at least a foot when everyone screamed: Surprise and *Felicidades*!

Before she could greet anybody, the whole house began a chorus of *Las Mañanitas*. Chabela, meanwhile, alternated between hugs, hands over her mouth, tears streaming down her face, and more hugs.

The women disappeared into the kitchen. Ray's daughters and Chabela and Jorge's nieces and nephews settled into games, and Nintendo. The men went out to the yard with beers in hand and stories to tell.

A neighbor of Chabela and Jorge, Raulito Reyes, brought over his guitar and began to sing. Ray couldn't help but laugh as he thought of Jorge describing Raulito.

"*Pues*, his name is little Raul, but you see, he is a very big man." And Jorge went on, "On the week-ends he often plays with a Mariachi band. But you got to see it, little Raul, the really big man, plays with the Mariachis, but he plays the little tiny *guitarrita*, and sometimes the mandolin. You gotta see him, a big man with a little tiny instrument."

Jorge almost rolled over laughing at this. He was fond of Raulito, but also enjoyed endlessly teasing him about these contrasts.

After a few beers, the men were called to the house to eat. Then, followed the children. The women stood around the kitchen supervising these feedings. Eventually, the women began to fill in chairs as men and children finished and moved on. The men went outside again and were joined by the women in short order. All began to tell *chistes*. Usually these jokes were pretty corny and known by everybody already. But this was the ritual, and everybody had a chance to tell their joke, and everybody roared with approval. Jorge, of course, always stole the show.

At last Raulito began to play again. The men all joined in as he sang, "*Con dinero y sin dinero, hago siempre lo que quiero y mi palabara es la ley. No tengo trono ni reina, ni nadie que me comprenda, pero sigo siendo el rey"*. The women groaned at this notorious anthem of machismo but joined in the chorus anyway.

The women went back inside to open the birthday gifts and the men began to get coffee. That was when Jorge gave Ray a special little signal to meet him back behind the garage. He looked like he was bursting to tell him something.

"*Compadre*, I've been waiting all night to get a chance to tell you. And Chabela is going to tell Lety, but we didn't tell anybody else yet."

"What's up, Jorge? Come on, *Compa*, you are smiling about something. Did you get a raise at work? Are you going to Cancun or something?"

Jorge waved his hand dismissively, still grinning from ear to ear.

"Ay no, *compadre*, this is way better than money or anything."

"Soooooo? What's up?"

"Chabela is going to have a baby, *compadre*."

Ray was in shock and stupidly, he thought later, asked, "But, *compadre*, how can that be? I thought the doctor said...I mean what happened? How did this happen?"

Jorge was laughing hard, "How did it happen? How do you think? The normal way, *compadre*!"

Ray was laughing now, too. He just gave his *compadre* a

big *abrazo*. Ray looked at Jorge again and said, "I can't believe this. I am so happy for you guys. I can't believe it."

"*Pues, así es la vida*," Jorge said as he shrugged his shoulders.

Ray couldn't believe what Jorge had just said. "*There is that Mexican thing again*," he said to himself. "*Así es la vida. I guess it is for the good things as well as for the bad things.*"

Later that night as they lay in bed, Lety turned to Ray and asked, "Did Jorge talk to you tonight?"

And answering a question with a question, Ray asked, "And did Chabela talk to you tonight?"

"Ramón, stop playing with me. Isn't it great news? I am so happy for them."

"Me, too, *amor*. I hope it will all go okay."

"I know it is going to be this time, Ramón. I know it is. Chabela even made a *promesa a la Virgen*. She is going to go down to La Villita at Guadalupe in Mexico and bring *La Virgen* a gold crown, if it all comes out right. And you know what she told me? If it is a boy, and Jorge agrees with her, they will call him Jesus after *La Virgen's* son. If it is a girl, they are going to call her *María de los Milagros*, but I think *Milagro* for short. Isn't that sweet?"

"Of course, it is." And Ray kissed Lety on the shoulder. "But you know, I can't figure it out. I asked Jorge: how did this happen? And you know what he told me? Ray leaned his body into Lety's and began to tickle her as he whispered into her ear: It happened the natural way."

"*Ay*, Ramón, stop it." she laughed.

"For real, Lety, he told me that. But I can't figure it out. You know the doctors say one thing, but maybe it is La Virgen or something, I can't figure it out."

Lety nibbled his ear and whispered, "*Pues, así es la vida, mi amor*".

They both laughed until their lips found each other's. They kissed and passionately made love.

The next day Ray got to the funeral home early to make sure all was ready for the Villaseñor wake. The first showing for the family would be at 1:00 p.m. Ray went into the parlor. Andy and Eddie had done a nice job. Ray was struck at the tenderness of the sight of the dead infant held lovingly by his dead mother.

At the viewing, the family seemed comforted. As the afternoon wore into evening most of the neighborhood must have passed through the funeral home. But what was striking is that there was rarely any sound from within the parlor, except for the gentle patting of the back as people gave deep abrazos to the family members.

Father Alex came at 8:00 p.m. to say prayers. As he stood in the doorway he said to Ray, "I have never seen a wake that is so, so quiet."

"*Padre*, it has been that way all afternoon."

They watched a while as the people in line moved toward the coffin, and then gave family members that silent *abrazo*. Now and then there was a muffled sob, but Tony Villaseñor,

133

his son, Junior, his three daughters, Patti, Salina and Lisa, and little six year old Frankie stood stoically in front of the coffin with their mother and baby brother in her arms.

The next day at the funeral mass Ray noticed this same stoic appearance. Ray kept thinking throughout the mass, "These folks must be more like *Indígenas*, than Mexicans."

At the cemetery Ray assisted the mourners to move toward the open grave. Chairs had been set up for the family, but Tony, and his children stood.

Fr. Alex led the prayers, "*Señor, ten piedad. Cristo, ten piedad. Señor, ten piedad*".

When he concluded the service, Ray stepped forward and gave the undertaker's usual spiel, "This concludes our cemetery service. On behalf of the Villaseñor family, we would like to thank you for your attendance here at St. Mary's Cemetery and to all those who participated in the beautiful funeral mass and paid tribute at the wake last night. We are grateful to Fr. Alex for his kind prayers. And now if the gentlemen pall bearers would place their gloves on the coffin we will conclude our service. *Damas y caballeros*, you may now all return to your cars."

But no one moved.

The cemetery workers arrived on the scene with the equipment for the burial. Still no one moved.

The workers began to slowly turn the cranks at each end of the coffin, and it slowly began to be lowered into the grave. Once it was down in the cement vault, Tony Villaseñor reached over to the pile of dirt to the side of the grave. He took one handful at a time and gave it to his children. He pulled little Frankie closest to him. No one spoke. Ray and Fr. Alex, the cemetery workers, all stood in place and could only watch. This was no longer their ritual.

Tony walked little Frankie to the edge of the grave and he let the earth fall from his hand. He held Frankie's hand, and let the dirt fall onto the lid of the coffin.

Tony then said to Frankie, *"Mi hijo"*, and then looked to each of his children one by one, and went on, *"¡Mira y nunca olviden!* Look and never forget!"

Each of his children in turn walked over to their father and standing next to him let the earth fall from their hands. Soon, in silence, the other mourners joined in the same gesture. Fr. Alex was the last to complete this gesture. Then Ray signaled the cemetery workers to seal the grave.

As they did their final work, no one else moved.

Finally, Fr. Alex blessed the grave and himself and pointed to the other mourners to move toward their cars. Ray stood for a moment with Tony Villaseñor and his children. A single tear ran down Rudy's cheek.

Finally, with his arm around his son, Tony Villaseñor looked at Ray and said only, *"Así es la vida"*.

El Grito de Dolores

THE WHOLE MEXICAN COMMUNITY in Chicago was buzzing about this year's celebration of Mexican Independence Day. This year, instead of multiple neighborhood activities, there would be one massive city-wide celebration in Millenium Park on the night of September 15th. The Consul General of Mexico would be on hand to give the traditional *Grito de Dolores*. There would be a big parade the following day along Columbus Drive through the park.

Fifth grader, Marco López, couldn't have been more excited. His dad had been talking about the event for weeks now. He had already made plans to switch from his night shift with a friend at work so he could make sure his children could be part of the celebration. He was fond of reminding Marco and his brothers that they were all *"ciento por ciento Mexicanos."*

Marco was on his way to serve the 8:30 a.m. school mass and as he was leaving the house his mom called him back for a minute.

"Mi hijo, trae estos anuncios para el padre y las madres." Like her husband Gustavo, Cuca López was excited about the upcoming celebration and she wanted to make sure the priests and nuns knew they were invited along too.

Once in the sacristy and dressed in his cassock to serve mass, Marco stood silently fingering the flyers announcing the big event. He noted they were in Spanish on one side and English on the other. Fr. Ryan came into the sacristy and began to vest for mass and as he did so he noticed Marco standing quietly to the side holding something in his hands.

Ryan knew that Marco was raised in a very traditional Mexican family and would never be so bold as to speak to him first. Ryan had grown up in an Irish family and, so, long ago had learned the ways of indirect communication. He thought of his grandfather, Eamonn Farrell who always seemed to answer a question with a question. When Jim Ryan came for his first visit home from the seminary, he remembered asking Grampa Eamonn if it was true the Irish always did answer a question with a question. Grampa Eamonn simply said: "And who told you that?" Another memory came to mind quickly. One year before at Christmas dinner, the gathered adult relatives were enjoying a "bit of the creature," as they called it. Grampa Eamonn sat with an empty glass. Rather to die a thousand deaths than to ask for some more directly, Grampa Eamonn simply said, "Oh now that was a fine drop."

Uncle Jackie jumped up with big eyes, "Oh God, Eamonn, what an omadhuan am I. Would you have some more?"

"Well, I wouldn't say no," retorted Grampa Eamonn with a little grin, glad that once again indirection saved face for himself and allowed Uncle Jackie to recover being the gracious host.

Growing up with that among his Irish relatives, Ryan found, was great preparation for working in the Mexican community. *"Indirectas"*, is what the Mexicans called it. *"God, they're just like us Irish,"* Ryan thought more than once. He had come to be able to interpret some key expressions. When the choir members straggled in late for practice for the Holy Week services, Ryan had given the group a strong rebuke.

"Now tomorrow we start at 7:00 p.m. sharp. And I expect everybody here." And to underline his seriousness, and perhaps to let show some of his irritation, he went one by one around the room pointing to and calling each by name," Carlos, you will be here at 7:00 p.m. right?"

"Sí, padre." "Gabriel?" "Julián?" "Dora?" "Cosme?"

Each responded *"Sí, padre."*

And then he came to Tomasa, *"Sí padre, si Dios quiere"*. "Yes, Father, if God wills it." There it was: the'yes', but 'no.

No one would ever say no to the priest, except, of course, God himself. In the end while the *indirectas* sometimes hooked Ryan's American efficiency, it mostly endeared these folks to him, not so different from "his own."

So with Marco he took the lead.

"Marco, how are you today?"

"Good, *Padre.*"

But it was clear from the way Marco was fidgeting he was waiting to be asked more.

"So, how are your mom and dad and your family?"

"Fine, *padre.*"

"Well," thought Ryan," that is not what's on his mind."

"Marco, what have you got there?"

Marco lit up," *Padre*, my mom told me to bring you these papers."

"What are they about?" Ryan took a flyer.

"Our whole family is going, *padre*. We are all going to hear the '*grito*.' And my dad wants to invite you and the other *padres* and *las madres*. It's going to be fun and we get to stay up to midnight to hear the '*grito*'"

"The *grito*, the scream, the shout?" Ryan was puzzled about what the *grito* was.

"Marco, let me take some of these. I will give them to the sisters, and I will put some in the back of church."

Ryan thought, "*I better look into this. Maybe we should put it in the bulletin, too, if this is something big for the community.*" He turned to the lad and pledged, "Marco, I will talk to Father Figueroa about this, too,"

"Ok, *Padre*, but he is Puerto Rican. But he can come, too"

"I am sure he will be happy to know that," Ryan smiled.

Later in the day Ryan had a chance to read the flyer more carefully. He still didn't know what the "*grito*" meant. Did it mean scream? Shout? He googled "*grito*" and up popped all kinds of references. Officially, it was called "*el Grito de Dolores*" before going further, Ryan thought, "*My Spanish is pretty good. If I am not mistaken this means literally 'the scream of sorrows, or wounds, or grief.'*"

But he read on. *"El Grito de Dolores"* referred to proclamation of independence, a shout: *"¡Qué viva la Independencia! Qué viva México!"* This cry was uttered by Father Miguel Hidalgo, a Catholic priest, from the pulpit of his church in a little town called Dolores in the Mexican state of Guanajuato.

For Ryan the significance was getting clearer. "Half of the Mexicans in this parish are from Guanajuato," he thought. "This is one of the most strongly Catholic parts of Mexico. No wonder the López's hope the priests and nuns will come. This is totally about identity—Mexican and Catholic."

At dinner in the rectory that night, Ryan shared all this with Fr. Figueroa, the other associate pastor, and Fr. Hayes, the pastor.

"Maybe we should organize a caravan from the parish to go," said Fr. Figueroa.

"Let's put this in the bulletin", added Fr. Hayes.

Ryan shared his first interpretation.

"El Grito de Dolores—you know at first I was thinking this is the scream or shout of sorrow or grief. And I'm like: what kind of celebration is this? But now I get it. It's pretty cool a priest is in the middle of this. It's all about this priest leading Mexico 's independence from Spain."

"He'd probably get excommunicated today," chimed in Fr. Hayes.

"I think he was," added Fr. Figueroa, "after all the Catholic Church and Catholic Spain were pretty much the same thing."

140

"So what did the Cubs do today?" asked Fr. Hayes, not so indirectly changing the subject. He was one of the old labor priests, and not afraid of a good fight for justice. But he wasn't as into the theology of liberation as Fr. Figueroa was. Fr. Hayes was one of those priests who fought pretty hard to keep any hint of anything Marxist out of the Labor Movement.

For Fr. Figueroa it was a different story. He had grown up in the Puerto Rican community, both on the Island and here in Chicago. He was sympathetic to the cause of Puerto Rican independence. Independence and the expression of faith, he felt, gave people a sense of identity. He was getting excited about the possibilities of making Mexican Independence Day a parish event. His excitement allowed him to pass on Fr. Hayes' bait. Ordinarily trying to change the subject on touchy issues, which Fr. Figueroa thought the Irish did way too often, would get a rise out of him. Tonight he was thinking ahead.

And so he answered, "The Cubs dropped two runs to the Cardinals in the 8th inning. I am afraid the Billy Goat's curse continues."

The next day, Ryan spoke to Sister Mary Ann, the school principal. And she, too, thought it would be a good idea to get the parish involved in the celebration.

The following Sunday, Fr. Figueroa talked about the upcoming Mexican Independence celebration in his homily at the English mass.

"This is an important event for the Mexican members of our community. Here in Chicago and in this parish we come from so many different places. We are Mexican, and German, and Puerto Rican. We are Irish and Polish, African-American and Asian, male and female, married and single, straight and gay. Each of us should claim our identity, the identity God gave us. And we should celebrate that identity. But here we are one church, the Mystical Body of Christ, we become one community. We stand in solidarity with each other. We treasure each other. We learn from each other."

He went on to announce that San Silvestre would be organizing busses to take parishioners down to the Mexican Independence Day celebration to hear the *"Grito de Dolores"* and he urged everybody, especially if they weren't Mexican, to stand up and show their solidarity and join the celebration. It was a rousing sermon.

Among those listening to it were Chris Mahon and Nicanor Castillo. They had been lovers since they first met last May. So much had happened in that time. Nico realized his dream to open an art studio, a place, as he said, "filled with beautiful things." He was painting and already selling some canvasses. Chris was realizing a dream, too. He had never been happier. He loved Nico more than he ever thought possible. Every day was a happy adventure.

Sitting in church this morning Chris still had painful memories of his decision to leave the seminary because he could not embrace his vocation and his same sex attraction, as they called it. He walked away from the church with a lot of bitterness. It was Nico who urged him to go to church. And Chris still couldn't believe how everything seemed to have changed.

"Nico, did you just hear what the priest said? He mentioned gay people and the need to claim and celebrate our identity. I can't believe it!" Chris whispered with a shocked look on his face. "I love this guy."

"I told you, Chris. It's beautiful here, really," Nico whispered back.

As he did so he discreetly reached over and squeezed Chris' hand. Chris' old instinct to hide anything spontaneous like this had long gone. He did not move his hand but looked at Nico. Nico looked back and they both smiled. Celia Claus saw this from her angle at the end of the pew in front of the boys. She caught their eyes, smiled, and bowed her head slightly.

After mass, walking home, Chris said, "Nico, that priest, Fr. Figueroa, was wonderful. He just made me want to be part of all this again."

"Chris, do you want to go to the Mexican Independence fiesta? It could be nice if everybody is gonna be there. Like a big party at the lake. And you heard the father: everybody is welcome. But only one thing I don't like—that *grito*. When the father said the *Grito de Dolores*, all I could think was the scream of grief, like somebody in terrible pain. It made me "*tiritar*", you know, shake inside."

"Well, yea, I thought that was a weird thing, too. I thought my Spanish was off. But it made sense when he said it was a shout for independence and from a priest. And Dolores was just the name of the town."

"Well, I think we should go."

September 15th came sooner than everybody thought.

At San Silvestre Fr. Figueroa was well organized. Five yellow school busses waited in front of the church for those going to the city's Mexican fiesta in Millenium Park.

The López family were the first waiting on the church steps. Gustavo, Cuca and their five children were a fine display. Marco and his brothers were wearing the big Charro hats one might associate with Mariachis. Cuca and her daughters had colorful skirts, and rebozos and their hair was pulled back tightly.

Teen daughter Angie shouted to her friends who were gathering, "Hey you guys, why are you going like *pachucas*?", a slang word for tough street girls. "Look at us, we're *chinitas poblanas*", and she bowed gracefully like a ballerina. The whole gathering crowd broke out with laughter at this exchange.

The Flores' were the first of the Puerto Rican families to arrive. Fr. Figueroa has worked hard to turn out the Puerto Ricans. Soon others arrived.

Celia Claus decided not to go because it would be so late coming home. But a number of the other old German ladies were there.

Chris and Nico arrived. Chris recognized the lesbians who owned the book store with their little boy. Chris turned to Nico to point them out, but Nico had big eyes and that huge grin of his. He nodded down the block. There was a whole delegation of clearly gay men making their way toward the busses.

And kids. Kids were running around everywhere.

144

Fr. Jim Ryan was out front there, too. He seemed to know most of the young families and all the kids.

In all these months since coming back to church, Chris had not remembered that Jim Ryan was at this parish. He saw him at a distance and thought, *"Hey I know him."* And his stomach went into a knot. Jim had been several years behind Chris in the seminary. They did not know each other very well. It wasn't Ryan that caused the knot in his stomach. He just reminded Chris of his painful journey at that time and place. He was amazed, after these past happy months, how quickly the bitterness stirred. With Nico's love, Chris began to recognize these feelings more as grief, and a kind of sadness at something lost and beyond recovery. *"My own little grito de Dolores,"* Christ thought in that moment.

"Do you know that father?" Nico asked.

"Yes, we were in the seminary around the same time. But I haven't seen him for a long time. I forgot he was in this church. He is a nice guy."

"You gotta say hello, *papi*," Nico said with that look of his that never took no for an answer. So Chris did.

He introduced Nico to Fr. Ryan, too. He couldn't believe it was him speaking as the words came out of his mouth, "Jim, Chris Mahon. I forgot you were at this parish."

"Chris, I thought that was you but I wasn't sure. It's been a few years. I didn't know you lived in the neighborhood"

"Yes, for a few years now over on Hudson. Jim, this is my partner, Nico."

Chris had claimed Nico in public and to a priest. Chris was almost giddy. He had done it and there was no longer a knot in his stomach. Nico was, of course, elated.

Jim Ryan simply said, "It is so nice to meet you." And then he engaged Nico more fully, "So are you Mexican or Puerto Rican?"

"Oh no, I am from Nicaragua."

"Have you been in Chicago long?"

Chris was sure that that same beguiling smile and those drop dead Latino good looks that first snared him were somehow working their charms on the young Fr. Ryan. "Aha", thought Chris, big bobby pins getting dropped here. Fr. Ryan's enthusiastic engagement of Nico made him want to shout, Hello, I'm another person in the world", one of his favorite lines from Torchsong Trilogy.

"How long have you guys been together?" Fr. Ryan asked now including Chris back in the conversation.

Chris once again could not believe that the words were coming from his mouth, "For the five happiest months of my life." Nico put his arm through Chris.

"Oh, that's wonderful, guys," said Ryan.

Chris was dumfounded. His fragmented worlds had just collided. What he had feared, what had so often paralyzed his feelings, had just happened. He not only survived the moment, but he was overjoyed, alive, whole.

"Nico, this parish is incredible," he said as the busses pulled away from the church. "And you are the one who brought me here. You know something you are just the best. You are something beautiful. I love you so much." Nico just smiled.

As they got closer to Millenium Park, Nico got quiet.

"Nico, what's up? You are *pensativo*."

Chris knew Nico enough to know when he was quiet all of sudden, he was mulling something over, something intuitive, something vague.

"I don't know, Chris. I think it's that *Grito* de Dolores. You know it is *doble sentido*, like you said before. Is it the shout of Dolores Hidalgo, or is it the scream of sorrows?"

Chris let the question hang in the air for a minute.

"But let's have a good time. This is a special *fiesta*," said Nico, his happy humor returning.

Meanwhile on the Southside, the Ayala brothers and the other vatos in the Playboys gang were also getting ready to celebrate Mexican Independence Day. Since this was the first year everything got moved downtown, everybody was going to be on territory the Kings claimed was theirs.

But César Ayala told his crowd, "Tonight we're gonna let the Kings know that we own Chicago."

The war between the Kings and the Playboys had heated up all summer. Thirty –eight young people had already been caught up in the violence in neighborhoods on both the North and South sides. San Silvestre had seen its share of deaths already. It had gotten so bad on the Southside that three teen aged gang bangers were gunned down on the steps of a church. There was a strange religiosity among gangbangers. They could be in the middle of a chase, but when they passed a church, they always seemed to stop and bless themselves before taking up the chase again. On that one occasion the Playboy pursuers caught up to the three Kings still blessing themselves and cold bloodily gunned them down. The drive by shootings had escalated and as innocent little children were gunned down it truly rocked the city. The gun down on the church steps was just about the last straw.

Tonight the Kings knew one of the biggest events for the city would be held at Millenium Park. Tonight's event was the Latino event of the year for the city. And it was on King's turf. But their leaders, guys with names like, Too Tough, Eight ball, and Carnitas had given orders that nothing should happen near that park.

"The Five-o is all over this, man," Carnitas said. if anything, the Kings were known for their discipline. No Kings went anywhere near Millenium Park that night. But the Playboys were out on the prowl to make a name for themselves.

Father Figueroa had sent the Romo sisters and the Villagrana family down to the park early tom scope out a gathering place for the San Silvestre group. Wisely rather than take a Mexican flag to be their calling card, they took the banner of San Silvestre and a papal flag. Freddie López was the first to spot the white and gold papal flag, truly unique in a field of Mexican flags. The section they selected was right up along Lake Shore Drive so everybody also had a great view of lake Michigan from the San Silvestre camp site.

The program that night included Mariachis, and another group playing Mexican polkas. This was a favorite for the old German ladies, perhaps reminiscent of music from their homeland. In between acts there was music from Los Lobos, Juan Gabriel, Ana Gabriel, and, of course, Vincente "Cente" López. There were speeches by the mayor, a greeting from the Catholic archbishop, and from Rev. Samuel Rios who headed up the biggest Hispanic Pentecostal Congregation. Everything built up across the evening to the introduction of the Honorable Jose Luis Huitrado, the Consul General of Mexico.

He gave a long winded speech on the Mexican diaspora, and ended by saying, "*Tonight todos somos Mexicanos.*" A church bell began to ring loud and wildly, then the Consul General shouted, "*¡Mexicanos!*" The whole park seemed to roar to life.

"Mexicanos! long live the heroes that gave us the fatherland and liberty!" A roar came again from the crowd

"*¡Viva Hidalgo!*".

The crowd roared, "¡Qué viva!"

The Consul General worked through a litany of heroic names and finally shouted:

"*¡Mexicanos! ¡¡Viva la Independencia! Viva Mexico! ¡Viva Mexico! ¡Viva Mexico!*"

A half a million people were on their feet shouting: "*¡Viva Mexico!*"

Gus and Cuca López were hugging their children. Fr. Figueroa had tears coming down his face. The delegation from Boys Town were tossing a petite young man up in the air and shouting: "¡*Qué viva!*" The Puerto Ricans were hugging everybody, and doing meringue moves and shouting "*Chévere!*" to everyone's delight.

The black Toyota with the shaded windows turned south onto Lake Shore Drive and took the lane closest to the sidewalk along the field where thousands were gathered for the Mexican Independence celebration. The driver was an eighteen year old with the nickname: Gleem, given because of his pearly white teeth. Also in the car with him was another eighteen year old named Abrigo, Overcoat, because he was always complaining he was cold. Finally, in the back seat carrying the automatic weapon was a seventeen year old called Pirata, or Pirate, because of the bandana he always wore on his head.

Gleem shouted: "*Ey, Pirata*, get ready. We are coming up to those mofos now. Let's teach the Kings a lesson."

Abrigo reached out the car window and made the Playboys rabbit hand gesture and shouted, "Playboys rule!"

Pirata adjusted the gun and made ready to shoot.

Fr. Ryan spotted Chris and Nico and came over and shouted, "So, this is *El Grito de Dolores!*" The noise was just deafening, and they could barely hear what he shouted. The mood was festive. They never heard the shots.

As Chris was leaning in to hear Fr. Ryan, Nico leaned into him, and then suddenly grasped the front of his shirt as he started to slide down Chris' chest. He thought Nico was playing, but he caught the total panic in his eyes and then

150

he saw the blood. With that he lowered Nico to the ground. "Chriii….." "Chriii…" he couldn't speak. His eyes riveting on Chris' and he kept grasping for Chris' hand. Chris held his hand even as he cradled his body as best he could.

Fr. Ryan leaned over Nico all ashen faced, but resolute. He made the sign of the cross over Nico and gave him absolution.

"Take care of him, Chris," he said as rushed over to see Cuca López cradling her youngest son, Ricky., a small bloodied Charro hat off to the side. He made the sign of the cross again.

David Martínez was pulling him next. "*Padre, padre, ven, ven,*" His wife, Chabela, was surrounded by parish ladies who had already placed one of the blankets from the picnic over her body.

Fr. Figueroa did everything he could to keep the other hysterical parishioners calmed. Alderman Rafa Reyes had been schmoozing with some other supporters when he noticed Fr. Figueroa gesturing to the crowd around him to kneel. Amidst shouts and tears, he began reciting the rosary,

"*Padre nuestro…Dios te salve, María…*" The rosary had a calming effect. To one woman who began to hyperventilate, the priest commanded, "Come on now, *Dios te salve, María….*" The woman began to breathe the words of the prayer both in and out until she calmed.

Mayhem broke out in the rest of the park, even as the San Silvestre crowd embraced their dead, sheltered their living, and continued to pray. The drive-by shooters killed seven in total, three of the dead were from San Silvestre.

The drive-by shooters were racing back to the Southside down Lake Shore Drive. They were pleased. They made their claim on the King's territory. And everybody would have to respect them now. This would mean a much bigger piece of "*la lana*" as they called it, "the wool," a cut in the drug trade. For now they disappeared into the night. Their bragging would take them to death row in a short time as the entire city demanded; ¡*ya basta*!

Chris held Nico. Nico's eyes were fixed on Chris and never left his gaze until finally with a brief sigh, they glazed a bit and closed. His grip let go of Chris' hand. Chris let out a scream, "Nico, no; Nico, no, no, no. Oh God, no, not Nico. Not now."

Cuca López just moaned for her son as her other children hung on to her for dear life. David Martínez sobbed and kept mumbling softly, "Chabela, Chabela."

The San Silvestre group kept vigil with their dead ones until the paramedics finally took them away. Still no one would leave the park. It seemed like hours passed. Finally Fr. Figueroa and the young Alderman began moving the parishioners toward their buses.

Fr. Ryan was the last to leave. Before he did though, he scanned the now almost empty park. He felt as though he were standing in a field after a battle. There was litter, and abandoned coolers, and chairs and blankets- the detritus of a panicked crowd. What had been a place of such joy and pride such a short time ago was a field of death. And in place of the rhythm and sound and energy of Latin music there was a terrifying silence all brought because of "*El Grito de Dolores*."

Ryan could not help but reflect to himself, "Tonight the *grito* is no longer *doble sentido*. Tonight it does not refer to a proclamation of independence uttered by a priest so long ago. Tonight el *grito* is "The scream of grief."

Héctor's Dream House

SERGIO WATCHED AS HIS FATHER carefully put the cardboard house back up on top of the cabinet. Up there it was safe from the horseplay of Sergio and his brother, Héctor. Héctor was named for his father, but he was always just called Junior.

"*Pa*, the house is safe with me. Junior is *más juguetón*."

"*Ni modo*," replied Héctor senior. "You two are always clowning around and you better not break my *casita*."

The cardboard house was Héctor senior's pride and joy. He had dreamt for years about going back to Celaya. And this cardboard house was the very model of the house he would build once they got back to Mexico.

Sergio looked up at the cardboard house again and remembered many evenings when his dad would come home from work looking tired. He would call his two sons to sit with him, and then with great care he would take down the cardboard house.

"*Mira, m'ijito*, here is gonna be your room. Junior, here is your room. Here is the room for mama and me. And here is the room for *mi mama*. *Hijos*, your *abuela* will be so happy to be with the two of you."

154

"Will she stay with us, *Pa*?"

"*Sí, sí*. She will live with us. I don't want her to be alone."

"She's always fun, *Pa*," said Sergio, knowing this would please his father to hear.

"*Hijos*, look, here is the little *jardín* behind the house. We can get some *gallinas*, and maybe a little *cabrito*, too."

"*Pa*, can we get a dog?"

"Yea, *Pa*, can we get a dog?

"*Sí, sí*. The dog can stay in the garden, too."

Héctor Miranda, senior, was a proud man, and one of few words. But when it came to his little cardboard house, he could go on for hours, and with an enthusiasm that always surprised his boys. That little cardboard house had been up on top of the cabinet for as long as Junior and Sergio could remember.

Each time they went through this routine they watched their work weary father light up and get excited. And each time they learned more about their family in Mexico. They heard tales of the rancho just outside Celaya, Guanajuato, where papa was born. Sometimes papa would sing a song or tell them funny stories about people with names like "El Moco", El Pedotes", "El Tortillero" and "La Alguendera." Always when *Pa* finished, the little cardboard house was tenderly picked up and placed back up on its safe perch.

As they grew older, though, Junior said to Sergio one night, "*Pa* looks like the priest at church holding up the communion."

Sergio laughed. He always laughed at Junior's wisecracks. But he thought, "But this is like a holy thing to *Pa*."

Watching his father repeat this reverent act one night, Sergio remembered a funny story about the house. "Papa, remember the time *Tío* Miguel brought his *gringo* friend here?"

Héctor senior chuckled as he remembered..

Junior chimed in, "Yea, *Pa*, remember. The *gringo* was all confused when he saw the house. He thought it was a doll house."

Sergio added, "*Pa*, he knew we were two boys, and he thought we had a doll house." Sergio giggled. Junior did too. And Héctor grinned broadly.

"Only a *gringo* would think this is a doll house, right, *Pa*?"

"*Ay pobrecito*," *Pa* added. "Maybe he thought you boys liked to play with dolls."

Both protested. "Naw, *Pa*, no way."

"He thought you had a doll house," said Junior with a bit of a smirk.

Héctor said nothing but gave Junior a stern look. The conversation was over.

As the boys had grown up that cardboard house was always above them on the cabinet. Héctor did not let them touch it. He seemed to get stricter about this as they got older. They were not to tamper with his dream house in any way.

Even their mother, Lety, would never move the house when she was dusting. Only Héctor himself would move the house.

Héctor would reprimand anyone who got too close to it. *"Mira, ten cuidado, la casa es frágil,"* he would growl.

As the years moved on Héctor was very protective of the little cardboard house. But his wife and sons could see that it brought him some inner joy.

One time when Junior was in seventh grade and Sergio was in fifth grade, they were tossing a little nerf football back and forth across the living room. The cardboard house sat above their field of play. When Héctor came in from work he exploded in anger at them. *"Hijos ingratos, sinvergüenzas,"* he shouted at them.

"But, *Pa,*" protested Junior, "we didn't get near the house!"

Héctor's eyes glowed, his nostrils flared, and he reared back to say something.

Sergio jumped in, *"Pa,* it's only a nerf ball, it can't...."

Héctor swung around to Sergio, *"¡silencio! No me respondas!* Both of you go to your room."

There was a cold silence for the remainder of that night.

The following morning Héctor was at the breakfast table when his sons awoke.

"Boys, come here. I want to talk to both of you." He went and carefully brought the cardboard house down from the cabinet top and placed it on the kitchen table.

"*Hijos,* I am sorry I was so mad at you last night," he began. It was a familiar lecture to them. "This is not just my house. This is the house I am going to build for all of us, for our family. You have to be more careful. This is our dream house."

In early September, Héctor received a call from Mexico with the news that his mother was very ill. His aunt had said she was "*muy grave.*" He left immediately for Mexico. He called each night with an update on his mother's condition. About two weeks after he arrived in Mexico, Héctor called to tell Lety, "*Ya se murió.* She is gone."

Héctor returned to Chicago about two weeks later. Lety and the boys found him silent and brooding. He would sit for hours in silence with his dream house, arranging and re-arranging things.

The boys who had never really know their grandmother that well were sad that they would never really get to know her better.

"She was always funny," Sergio told Junior. Héctor also knew that his sons would never really know their grandmother. And this truth stung deeply.

It was about this same time that Junior and Héctor began their arguments. Sergio was surprised sometimes by the strength of his brother's *rebeldía.*

"Junior, you are talking back to *Pa* a lot. You make him get angrier."

"I don't care, Sergio. He's not always right."

One night *Pa* threw a fit of rancor at Junior. Junior was playing music loudly.

"*Esa no es música*", shouted Héctor. "Turn it off, *apágalo*".

Junior retorted, "But, *Pa*, this is music we like. We don't like all those *rancheras* you like."

Héctor bristled and shouted at Junior, "*No seas respondón*. Don't you talk back to me."

Another night, Lety, Héctor and the two boys had been out shopping. Héctor suggested they stop for something to eat.

Sergio enthusiastically suggested, "let's go to McDonald's."

Héctor was quick to respond, "¡*M'ijo, eso no es comida buena!*"

But Junior couldn't resist jumping in, "*Pa*, it's the food we like."

Héctor flashed back, "Well, *no tienen* McDonald's en Celaya. There is no McDonald in Celaya."

But Junior had the bit in his teeth, "So what, *Pa* We don't even want to go to Celaya!"

Héctor was wounded and both boys knew it.

There was silence until Sergio tried to soften the air. "*Pa*, Celaya is beautiful. And we do love it, especially when we go in the summer. But, you know, all our friends are here."

Silence.

Finally, quietly but bitterly Héctor said, "You boys are *agringados*. You are nothing but *pochos*. I should never have brought you to this *pinche* country."

Without saying anymore, he pulled into McDonald's but would not get out of the car, nor would he order anything.

He said nothing for the rest of that night.

Sergio remembered these arguments went on all through their high school years. When Junior was a senior in high school, and Sergio was a sophomore, they were home one night eating a pizza. Héctor and Lety had gone out to visit their *compadres*. The boys were still eating when Héctor and Lety came home. Héctor seemed to have had a bit to drink. The boys looked at him and then at each other. Junior made a gesture to signify the old man had been drinking. Héctor caught the gesture out of the corner of his eye.

"You little *cabrón!*" he shouted at Junior. "And look at the two of you eating this *gringo* crap again."

Both braced for the argument that was coming. Lately it could be almost anything that would set Héctor off: music, dating, their friends, their haircuts, their earrings, their clothes, any of these were fair game for their father's *crítica*. All of these things were signs to Héctor that his sons were *gringos* pure and simple. And it was not just Junior who was talking back these days, but Sergio as well.

Tonight the argument was going to be about pizza.

"*Leticia, prepáreles algo de comer,*" Héctor ordered his wife. Looking at the pizza he added, "They haven't had any dinner."

"*Pa*, we're eating pizza. We're fine. Ma, it's okay. Don't make anything," Junior responded.

"*¡Esa no es comida buena!*" Héctor responded, his voice rising in a familiar refrain. The boys did not want to argue. they just wanted to eat their pizza.

"*Pa*," chimed in Junior," We are going over to Tigre's house and his mom always has more food over there."

"*¿A dónde vas?* You're not going out at this hour! *Ya es tarde.*"

"*Pa*, we don't have school tomorrow," added Sergio.

"*¡Les dije- no!*"

"*Pa...*", Junior tried to interject.

Héctor exploded.

"*¿Qué pasó con ustedes?* What kind of sons have you become? You have no respect. You talk back. Look how you dress. What are they going to say about you in Celaya? Everyone is going to talk about the two of you! ¡Pochos, *que no tienen respeto*! You two aren't even Mexican!"

These were fighting words.

"*Pa*, we're Mexicans! Don't ever say that. We love being Mexican! But we live here. our friends are here." Junior wouldn't drop it.

"Look how you talk back to me!" shouted Héctor.

But Junior was going to have the last word. "*Pa*, you are old fashioned! You're just out of it! ¡*Piensas Viejo*! You are not in Mexico now. We live here and we plan to stay here!"

With that Junior looked away from Héctor. He tried to change the subject and reached for a piece of pizza. But Héctor grabbed the pizza first. He grabbed the cardboard under the pizza and pulled it fiercely. With that pizza flew across the floor, but the cardboard under it went sailing through the air into the next room. Higher and higher it seemed to fly, and the whole family could see that it was on a direct line for the cardboard house on the top of the cabinet. It hit with a smack, and a corner of the house crashed to the floor with the pizza platter.

No one spoke. No one moved. Sergio watched as his father carefully picked up the pieces of his dream house. Héctor held the pieces in hands tenderly. It was an eternity. Finally, Héctor looked away from his broken house. He looked at his sons, first at Junior, then at Sergio, then at his wife Lety. All their eyes looked down. Héctor then, too, looked down and silently carried the broken house to his room. Anger had turned to feelings of shame.

The evening ended in silence.

Years later Sergio remembered that night. He remembered, too, the night he and Junior and Lety had returned from Mexico from Héctor's funeral. That night mama had Sergio bring down papa's dream house. Héctor had long ago patched it up. Lety took it into her bedroom. Many times, looking at the house, she thought of Héctor and his dream. But she also thought of her two sons and how they had come to have their dreams.

One cold Sunday afternoon some years later, Sergio and his *novia*, Irma, went to visit Lety. Junior and his family were already there. It still amazed Sergio that Junior and his wife, Maureen—yes, she was a gringa—already had two children. The oldest, Sally, was five years old. And Sergio found her with his mother back in her bedroom.

From the hallway he could hear his mother speaking to Sally. "Mira, Sally, here is something for you when you come here to play. Your *abuelo* and I always hoped we could have a little *nieta* who would come to our house to play. Here is a beautiful doll house for you. Your grandfather made it for you. But be careful with it. It is very fragile and easy to break."

Titi Belén

"*AY, NENA,* HURRY UP. We have to get going. We don't want Titi Belén looking for us all over the airport."

Daisy Flores was almost out of breath rushing her 12 year old daughter, Edie, and her seven year old son, Lito, out to the car. Nelson, her husband, was already out in the car waiting patiently, as he did so many times before.

With a grin, Nelson shouted to the breathless Daisy as she was about to get into the car: "*Apagaste la plancha?*" Daisy froze for a moment. Had she turned off the iron? "*Ay, Dio mío,*" she exhaled and started to turn to run back to the house. Nelson laughed out loud as did the two children, and Daisy, disgusted slid into the car.

"Ay, I wish Sonny and Danny didn't have to work. Titi Belén will be wondering why they're not with us", Daisy said still breathless.

"*Cálmate,*" Nelson added," Take a breath, woman. She'll understand." Nelson was always the calm in the any storm. And he had an easy relationship with Titi Belén. She always made him laugh. He knew she would be proud that his boys were out working. Nelson chuckled imagining Titi Belén's arrival.

"I hope we got enough room for her luggage. Remember the last time?" Nelson added. Daisy started to laugh.

"*Ay, Dio mío*, remember that? The one luggage weighed a ton!!" They both laughed hard as Nelson pulled away from in front of the house.

Daisy settled into a moment of reflection. Nelson, she thought, could never fully appreciate how important Titi Belén was for her. When her mother and father passed away, she was only 13 years old. And Titi Belén raised her during her crazy teenage years. While the whole rest of the world was always laughing in the presence of Titi Belén, Daisy knew her to be what the Puerto Ricans called "*una mujel fuelte*", one strong lady.

"Nelson, you know Titi Belén was like a mother to me. When *Mami* and *Papi* died she raised me. You know, "she said as she swung around to include Edie and Lito in the conversation, "she was strict with me. But now I appreciate how much she kept me on the right path in those years." Daisy smiled wistfully as she thought of her own teenage willfulness in those years. But much stronger was Titi Belén's will. "You kids think I take you to church too much, but you should have seen Titi Belén. I wanted to go out with my friends, but she made me go to church where everybody was singing and speaking in tongues and falling to the ground when somebody prayed over them. That stuff scared me. But at least she told the church people to back off, when I wanted to wear make-up.

Titi Belén had toyed with joining the *Iglesia Pentecostal*. She loved the excitement of their church services. But in the end she stayed with *La Católica* because they had La Visne,

165

the Virgin Mary, or as she called her "la Provi", short for the Virgin of Providence. Titi Belén found her spiritual home in the Catholic Charismatic Movement. She said it was the best of two worlds.

Daisy remembered the final line was drawn with the *Pentecostales* when they criticized Titi Belén for letting Daisy wear make-up. She told them: "My Daisy gotta look good so a nice man gonna like her." Daisy smiled at the remembrance and said to the kids, "Titi Belén was sure tough with me, but that was her business. She wasn't ever going to let somebody else tell her about her family. She's always been that way. You know, you guys, we always have to stick up for our family. She taught us that."

Turning to Nelson she added, "But Papi Chulo, she always liked you. For some reason, she always let you slide. You remember when we first started dating? And she wanted you to come to church with her."

Nelson grinned at the memory.

"I know. I told her I wasn't the church-going type. She came over with that big grin of hers and said, "*Ay, Dio mío,* then I'm going to pray for you." She kissed me on the head, and then blessed me.

Then she said, "Maybe I gonna bring the church to you one of these days," she said with a hearty laugh. "Daisy, you remembered how she laughed at that?

Daisy said, "Yea, she laughed out the door. So did we. But remember, I told you, one day you better be ready because she wasn't kidding."

166

In the back seat, Lito wasn't paying attention to this conversation. He seemed mesmerized by the trucks they were passing on the expressway.

But Edie was riveted. For her Titi Belén was a figure bigger than life. She knew Mami and Papi loved her. But no one could ever make her feel the way Titi Belén could. As the only girl in the family, it felt like Titi Belén singled her out for special attention. While her great aunt played, and teased her brothers, Titi Belén would always make her sit next to her at dinner, or on the couch when they were all watching tv. Titi Belén was always saying things like, "Mira, Nena, I gonna tell you somesing, but he's a secret. But you gotta promise to no say nussing to nobody."

Their relationship was always on the edge of conspiratorial. Titi Belén would tell Edie things about her family, and especially about the foibles of Edie's mother when she was growing up and was Edie's age. But what was most special to Edie was that when Titi Belén spoke to her brothers she always said: "*Ay, mi amor*," Oh my love. But when she spoke to Edie she always said, "*Ay, mi vida*", oh, my life. She couldn't wait now to see Titi Belén.

For another moment Edie held the image of Titi Belén. She was a full -figured woman with a round face, with round red cheeks, and round eyes, that became like saucers when she smiled or was excited. And she had a way of moving her mouth when she was talking about someone or something to point toward it. Her lips would pucker as if in a kiss, move to the side toward the object of her attention, and quickly point, so as not to get caught. Titi Belén would grin from ear to ear when she made this gesture. Edie had seen Titi Belén and the older Puerto Ricans make this gesture hundreds of times. It always delighted her.

"Here we are, and with plenty of time", Nelson said, interrupting Edie's thoughts.

They parked the car and made their way to the American Airlines baggage claim. As they walked Nelson turned to Daisy and said," I sure hope she doesn't have that big bag again." Nelson laughed playfully.

In the final moments of the flight, Titi Belén conjured an image of each member of the family: Daisy, whom she raised as her own and now the mother of four children. She thought of Nelson as that young man with his dark eyes and Puerto Rican good looks that Daisy first brought home. "He is a good man", she thought, "a good husband and father." Then she conjured an image of each of the Flores children. First there was Ezequiel Samson, whom everybody called Sonny. Then, came Isaiah Daniel, whom everybody called Danny. Then came Esther Judith, whom everybody called Edie. And finally, there was little Joel whom everybody called Lito from Joelito. She had insisted to Daisy and Nelson that each had to be baptized and they should have names from the prophets in *La Biblia*. Nelson naturally wanted his first born son to be Nelson Junior, but he knew he was not going to win that battle. His compromise was to give each child a nickname, something that would go down a little easier on Chicago's tough streets.

For Titi Belén this would be her first visit back to Chicago since she and so many of the old timers from San Silvestre moved back to Puerto Rico to get away from the cold

Chicago winters, and to hear the coqui one more time in their golden years. They all decided to come for the Fall. This was a beautiful time in Chicago. They would arrive a few days before Halloween and stay through Thanksgiving, or as they all called it: "*Sansgibby.*" For all of them this was always one of the best days of the year to be with family. Christmas was, of course, better, but it was just too cold anymore for Christmas in Chicago.

Titi Belén was traveling with Irma and Freddie Colón, her next door neighbors in Santurce now. On the plane there were also Lydia and Ramón Vázquez, and Nilda Sotomayor and her grandson Ricky.

Belén thought: "Tanks God, Nilda brought her grandson. *Esta bien nelviosa esa*".

Nilda was a nervous flyer and must have crossed herself 100 times as the plane rolled down the runway for takeoff. The flight attendant announced the landing in Chicago, "*Vamos a aterrizar en quince minutos.* We will be landing in fifteen minutes."

Freddie Colón shouted across the aisle to Nilda: "Nilda, vamos a 'terrorizar'!" He cackled amused with his little play on words. But Nilda was at it again: a hundred signs of the cross a minute.

Arriving at the baggage claim Daisy and Nelson found a sea of other Puerto Ricans waiting for the flight from San Juan. They heard the din before they saw the crowd.

"*Ay, Dio mio*".

"*Rafael, mira quién está aquí*".

169

"Ay, Commai".

Nelson swore half of San Silvestre had to be here. There were people hugging each other and children running around jumping on and off the conveyor belts. Old neighbors laughed. Finally the board lit up announcing the plane had landed. The crowd moved as one toward the bottom of the escalators. Everybody strained to be the first to spot someone they knew.

Edie stayed back from the crowd, standing alone, but near a group of bored teenagers. But she was anything but bored.

Someone shouted; "Ricky."

It was Yanira Mareno, who Edie knew a little bit from the neighborhood. She sometimes baby sat for her next door neighbors, the Aguilars. Obviously, she had a crush on Ricky Sotomayor.

Somebody else yelled: "There's Nilda Sotomayor."

Daisy first spotted Titi Belén. "Kids come on. Here comes Titi Belén! Nelson, Nelson, come on."

Titi Belén's face glowed as she came down the escalator.

"Ay, Daisy, mi nena. Ay, Nelson, tan guapo, like always."

Lito had run between the legs of the adults and planted himself right in front of Titi Belén . *"Ay mi Lito, mi amor"*, as she planted a big wet kiss on his cheek.

Edie held back for a moment. Titi Belén was scanning the crowd until she found Edie.

"¡*Ay Esther Judith. Edie, Edie. Ay mi vida!*" With those words Edie ran to Titi Belén and both starting crying with joy.

While the crowd waited for the luggage there was lots of commotion, and loud laughter, and lots of *bochinche*, as they say, catching up, gossip. Once again kids were running wild and most of the teenagers had retreated into boredom.

Edie, however, was in the firm grip of Titi Belén, and enjoying every minute of the attention.

Suddenly, Lito shouted out to Nelson, but for all to hear: "Papi, here come the bags."

And Nelson spotted the first huge oversized suitcase tumbling down the chute onto the carousel. Another of equal size followed this, and then another, and another. Nelson said to another man at the conveyor: "*Caramba*, they must only sell those big bags in Puerto Rico"

The other man laughed.

Another added: "I hope I got enough room in my car."

Another elderly man said, "They must got half of Puerto Rico in there."

Titi Belén shouted to Nelson, "My bag has orange tape on it. I made it like a cross," she beamed, grinning from ear to ear.

Lito spotted it first and Nelson rushed to get into position to grab it.

"Oh my God", he groaned at the weight of the bag.

He couldn't get it off the conveyor at first and so ran to the other end to intercept it. Thanking God, it had wheels on the bottom, Nelson maneuvered the bag toward the crowd of Puerto Ricans.

"Titi, this weighs a ton", he laughed.

"Oh, that's because I brought some *regalitos*." and turning to Lito, said: "For you, *mi amor*", and then turning to Edie, "And for you, too, *mi vida*."

The trip back home went by in a flash. Sonny and Danny were at the house waiting for Titi Belén.

"¡*Ay, Ezequiel, mi amor*! Sonny, Sonny", she shouted as she squeezed Sonny. It was Danny's turn next. "*Ay, Isaias, Danny, mi amor*."

The next few days were as joyful as the Flores family could remember.

One night Titi Belén, Daisy, Edie, Lito and Nelson were watching tv after dinner. There seemed to be nothing but ads for Halloween: Halloween candy, Halloween costumes, Halloween movie specials. Some ads featured ghosts, and worse, demons and devils of different kinds.

Sonny and Danny were having fun at everyone else's expense pulling pranks to scare them. They scared Lito so much one night he cried and would not be consoled. They then turned their sites on Edie. But like the Pentecostals with Daisy, the two brothers had crossed the line.

"*Bendito sea Dio*", Blessed be God," shouted Titi Belén. She turned fiercely but lovingly on Sonny, "*Mi amor*, you don't suppose to play with these things." She was wagging her finger, a rare gesture for her. "*Esa es brujería, cosas del demonio.*" She blessed herself and said: "*Santa Virgen, perdónalos*".

As fast as lightning she was marking Sonny on the forehead with the sign of the cross. "*Danny, mi amor, ven acá*".

Danny came over to her and she repeated the gesture on his forehead.

Danny was always the playful one and so he protested: "But, Titi, we're just messing round. It's not for real. We're not serious."

Not to be put off Titi Belén said firmly: "You think you just playing, but God sees you and He don't like this. You letting *los espíritus inmundos* come in this house. This Halloween *es pura porquería*! Don' you play with this ting. You pray God send the Holy Spirit and kick out the bad spirits."

Sonny got serious and said, "Titi, we are Catholic. We don't really believe in ghosts and goblins and that weird stuff."

But undeterred Titi Belén challenged Sonny. "In da bible it say we got angels, and some become a devil. *Mi amor*, the only thing you do with the bad spirit *es reprenderlo*. You don't make a funny about it. Tomorrow I gonna go to San Silvestre and pray God he watch over you and da whole family."

The next day was Halloween. Daisy could hear Titi Belén walking through the house from room to room. Curious she went to see what she was doing. Titi Belén had picked up *óleo santo*, blessed oil at the *círculo de oración* as well as a small bottle of *agua bendita*. She was going from room to room anointing the walls with oil, and sprinkling the corners with holy water. Daisy tiptoed away knowing to leave well enough alone.

Later that day the next door neighbor, Lourdes Aguilar, invited Daisy and Titi Belén over for coffee. Lourdes and Benjamín Aguilar were originally from Mexico. They had been good friends and neighbors since they moved next door.

As Titi Belén entered the house she noticed the family photographs on top of the tv set. Among the photos was one of two nuns in their old fashioned habits. Lourdes caught Titi Belén looking at the photo. "Those are Benjamín's two sisters back in Mexico."

"*Ay, que* nice", Titi Belén said. "What a blessing to have two *madres* in your family."

Lourdes responded," Benjamín's family *son muy católicos*, very Catholic. His grandfather and his brothers were *Cristeros* in the old days. Two of his grandfathers' brothers became *santos*. They were killed for *Cristo Rey*."

Titi Belén blessed herself, as she said, "*Ave María Purísima*." Instinctively both Lourdes and Daisy responded without thinking, "*sin pecadò concebida*".

Lourdes showed the ladies to sit in the dining room as she went to get the coffee. That's when Titi Belén noticed something very alarming. On a server in the dining room there was what looked like a small altar and most disturbing on it was a cake in the form of a skeleton. Without saying a word, Titi Belén caught Daisy's eye, and pursing her lips in that Puerto Rican gesture, pointed with her pursed lips to the skeleton cake.

Her eyes opened wide, and in a whisper she asked Daisy, "*¿Qué e' eso?*"

Then she noticed more: candy skulls and tombstones made of marzipan. There were black candles, and a shot glass filled with what she thought might be *ron caña*, the Puerto Rican moonshine you can get back in the mountains near San Lorenzo. And photos…there were photos.

Titi Belén was not able to hide her horrified look fast enough as Lourdes came into the dining room with the coffee.

Lourdes put the service on the table, look at Daisy with a smile, and then said, "*Titi Belén, no te preocupes de esa.* Don't worry about this. We are good Catholics. This is just an old Mexican custom to remember our *amados difuntos*, our dead ones. This is for the Feast of the Souls, the day after the Saints feast."

Titi Belén was intrigued.

Lourdes went on," We don't celebrate Halloween, like the *Americanos*. That is a pagan day. *Nos parece algo del Diablo.* So, in Mexico we think of all our dead family and we pray for them. The cake is for death, but it is a sweet cake, because Jesus *resucitó*. We pray our dead family get to get raised from the dead with Jesus."

Titi Belén was deeply moved. She had never seen this custom before.

"In Puerto Rico, you know, when somebody die, we have the *rosario* for nine nights. Then we have the mass for them maybe one month, and one year from when they die."

Daisy added, "Titi, you remember the Polish lady who used to live near us. She told us in their church the priest puts a coffin by the altar on the day for all souls and the people write the name of their dead ones and they put money in an envelope for the mass. They put it in the little coffin."

They all agreed these were much nicer customs than Halloween. Lourdes poured the coffee and they went on talking about their families and the news in the neighborhood.

As November wore on, the days seemed to get a little darker each day, and each day started to get a little colder. Titi Belén ran into some of her traveling companions at San Silvestre one Sunday and all agreed November in Chicago was a little colder than they had remembered. They were all looking forward to *Sansgibby*, Thanksgiving. It would be a great day for family, and its passing would be the signal for this flock to head back to La Isla del Encanto.

Titi Belén began to notice the signs of Thanksgiving: drawing of pilgrims and turkeys hung with magnets on the refrigerator door. Daisy bought a wreath and some dry floral arrangements with leaves of brilliant fall colors from a lady at work.

Strange to Titi Belén was that Daisy and Nelson, and every one of the kids kept referring to Thanksgiving as Turkey Day.

One day she heard Edie use this term, *"Mi vida,* what is this Turkey Day? Why you call it Turkey Day? He's *Sansgibby."*

On another occasion Daisy and Nelson both referred to Turkey day. Again Titi Belén said, *"Mi amor,* he's *Sansgibby.* Why you want a Turkey Day?"

Nelson tried his best." Titi, the kids all call it Turkey Day. For them it's a celebration that this is a great country. I mean we are not about the pilgrims and all that Yanqui stuff. But it's for the kids."

Titi Belén was not buying this. *"Mi amor,* I cane fron Puerto Rico, too. But when I cane here they told me it was *Sansgibby.* We suppose to say Sanks God on that day for all the good thing, and for the good life we got over here. How is Turkey Day say Sanks God?"

Titi Belén said all this in a voice a bit louder than usual. She was aware that younger ears were listening in on this conversation from the living room.

"Daisy, you remember. We always made a nice party for *Sansgibby.* We make *pernil asado, tostones, arroz con gandule, habichuelas,* ham and potato salad. Remember, we make a nice party and everybody come over?"

"But Titi, that is so much work. So we get the turkey breast, cranberry, and yams. It's nobody's favorite, but, hey. Titi, it's Turkey day. So we have it."

"You don't even make potato salad? What kind of Puerto Rican doesn't make potato salad when you make a party?" "And how you suppose to Sanks God with food you don't even like?"

A day or two passed before the subject came up again.

"Daisy, *mi amor,* we gonna have *Sansgibby,* but we gonna Sanks God. And I told the priest from San Silvestre, he gotta come because we gonna make a party."

"But Titi, we were just gonna have turkey for Turkey Day," protested Daisy.

"You don't worry, I gonna make it. Forget Turkey day, we gonna Sanks God the right way. We gonna have *Sansgibby.*"

Titi Belén got busy. She visited all the old markets along with a number of her traveling companions. She had to make sofrito first. She had to pick up the pernil and get the seasoning, and all the other Puerto Rican delights. And, she got the makings for her homemade potato salad.

The day before Thanksgiving, Titi Belén ran into Lourdes Aguilar out in front. *"Hola, m'ija"*, Titi Belén saluted Lourdes.

Lourdes was surprised to see Titi Belén carrying so many grocery bags. *"Ay Dios"*, she said, "You must be making a big party."

Titi Belén's face lit up. It went round. Her cheeks went round, and her eyes were again like huge saucers.

"Oh, bendito, yes. We gonna make a nice party for *Sansgibby.*"

She shared her conversations with Daisy and Nelson about Turkey Day and why it had to be Thanksgiving. "You know everybody want to forget this day is for Sanks God. We don't care we not Pilgrims and all those people. But they were right to make the day for Sanks God. I told Daisy how you can Sanks God with food you don't like? So we making a big Puerto Rican party."

Lourdes was thrilled to hear all this from Titi Belén.

"Titi, what you said is beautiful. In my family we have turkey for the kids. But I make it Mexican. I make a nice mole sauce. So we have turkey with *mole poblano*. It's a lot of work but I grind the spices myself. I make everything fresh like that. And we have tortillas and rice, and pintos. That's beautiful what you said: how can you thank God with food you don't like?"

"Lourdes, you know what. You should make a party with us. We got to show our beautiful young people about *Sansgibby*. But we make a Mexican and Puerto Rican *Sansgibby*." Titi Belén was grinning again from ear to ear.

The entire idea thrilled her. Her enthusiasm was contagious, and Lourdes said: "I will tell Benjamín tonight when he comes home. He will like this idea very much- a real *Sansgibby*"

On Thanksgiving Day, Nelson, Sonny, Danny and Lito were sent to San Silvestre to pick up the folding tables and chairs. Fr. Figueroa could not resist Titi Belén's request. He was kind enough to include a box of the left over white plastic wedding runners from church. Every church event used these for table cloths. Titi Belén was pleased as punch.

The Aguilar's arrived carrying what looked like a full Mexican buffet. The ladies took the food and got busy in the kitchen. The men settled down for beers and football. When Fr. Figueroa arrived everybody made their way to the basement where the tables and chairs had been set up. The tables were covered with a veritable feast. Titi Belén was in her glory.

"*Ay, Dio mío*, I almost forgot the potato salad. Edie, *mi vida*, can you bring it down?"

When Edie returned with the potato salad, Titi Belén placed it ceremoniously on the table, and said to one and all: "Ok now we can have 'appy *Sansgibby*. So sanks God everybody."

"I'll be Home for Christmas"

"I LOVE THIS TIME OF YEAR," Felix Muench said out loud to nobody in the empty house. He caught himself rather self-consciously and then whispered the next words. "There is nothing like Christmas in this city!"

Felix, who had never married, lived alone now in the large city Greystone where he had lived with his parents all his life, until they passed away within two months of each other over ten years ago. They were both ninety-six years old at the time of their deaths. His mother and father were born in Germany just at the end of the Great War in 1918. They were babies when they migrated but grew up knowing each other in the tight knit German neighborhood on Chicago's near North Side. They married and opened their jewelry store shortly afterwards and for so many ways lived the American Dream. Their business was profitable. They bought the striking graystone home built by an earlier generation of German immigrants. The year 1893 was carved in the capstone above the third floor on the stone masonry.

Felix had never known any other home. At age seventy-two, its three floors were almost getting to be too much for him.

Talking out loud to nobody again he added, "Thank God for Mrs. Sánchez."

She was the Mexican lady he met at St. Monica's Church who came each day to help clean the house. Felix also enjoyed her presence in the rambling empty house.

At 9:00 this morning Felix heard the phone and answered. It was a call he was expecting.

"This is Karl at Denziger's nursery up in Mundelein, Illinois. Is this Mr. Muench?"

"Yes, and I am so glad to hear from you. I was expecting your call."

"Ja, all these years we still have the standing order. I was a little boy when your father first came to our nursery to pick his Christmas Tree. Your father and my father would go off in German. I think they knew people from the old country."

"Yea, my father, always enjoyed his visits with Herr Denziger."

"Ha,ha,ha. I have not heard my dad called that in a long time."

"Well you know how formal they were, the old Germans."

"Ja, so you're getting ready for Christmas now?"

"Yes, the living room is all set just waiting for the tree to take its place of honor."

"We'll deliver the tree on Tuesday, if that will be okay for you? About 11:00 a.m.?"

"That's perfect. *Danke schoen*.

"*Weider schoen*. You're most welcome. Thanks again for your business. See you Tuesday."

Since the call Felix had been sitting in the attic. As he went through the boxes of Christmas ornaments he found himself wrapped in nostalgia of Christmases past. He could not remember all seventy-two so well, but those he remembered were all happy memories.

He found himself thinking, "I am so glad mother and father preserved the old German Christmas traditions. They would be pleased", he thought, I carry it on."

He had already been to Geppert's to order the Christmas goose. He had already been to Schmeissing's to order Hassenpfeffer cookies, and for Christmas a Johannesbeer Sahne Torte. And he had been to Kunst's delicatessen to order herring, and other delicacies.

"It's a good thing I'm retired. The last few years this was exhausting. But now the tree is on its way," Felix said once again to nobody, but feeling excited about its arrival. "I better invite some people over to eat all this food I ordered."

Felix went down to the kitchen when he noticed the time.

"Oh, I better get a move on. I've got to open the Church."

Since he sold the jewelry story and retired, Felix volunteered at St. Monica's Church on Saturdays as an usher. As he walked the three blocks to St. Monica's Felix verbally and out loud went over everything he had to take care of this afternoon.

"OK, let's see. First, I need to set up for the 5:30 p.m. mass. Do I have the combination to the safe? Oh, yes, I have my wallet. It's in the pouch there. Then I'll need to check to put the heat on. Next, I'll need to put the bulletins on the back tables. I hope they delivered them to the church this time, and not the priest house."

Felix unlocked the front door of St. Monica's when he arrived. And he set about his tasks. "But where are the bulletins?" he asked to nobody in the empty church.

"Here they are, Felix, I've got them."

For a moment Felix thought some ghost, or maybe an angel was answering him. But with that Fr. Von Ackerman, the retired pastor, came into the sacristy his arms heavy with the box of bulletins.

"I wish they would deliver these to the church instead of to the rectory," said Fr. Von Ackerman. "These are getting too heavy for old men like us, Felix."

Felix had known Fr. Ackerman as long as he could remember.

"Father, I got the call today from Denziger's nursery. The tree is on its way," Felix said smiling.

"*Sehr gut*, Felix, you are loyal. You know, I am retired so I shouldn't say anything here. You know I am not pastor anymore. It's a new day. Things are changing. Our new pastor said they have to follow the fire codes now so all the trees are fake trees. But can you imagine our old Germans without real trees and real candles burning on them? And for thirty five years I got the best trees from Denziger's and we never had one fire. You know the old man Denziger was a friend of my father's."

"Of my father, too," added Felix.

"Felix, in the old days all the old Germans knew each other. There was a real sense of Gemeinschaft, you know, community. I think that made it easier for them when they first came over and the those during the two wars,. They found their food, their newspapers, their churches, and their beer when they stayed in the community."

"And don't forget how they kept Christmas, Father. I remember as a little kid learning all the *Weichnachtsleid*. We sang them in school and at church on Christmas day. And all the special Christmas food. People felt really at home."

"You know, Felix, I worry about young people today. I don't think they feel very much at home any place. You see them walking down the street in this neighborhood now with earphones on or looking at their phones. It seems to me they don't have any community to belong to, like we did. Today it is community through electronics. To me that is fake community. And now we have to have fake Christmas trees!"

Felix got quiet for a moment, and then said," Father, you know me. I keep all the old German Christmas traditions. Sometimes doing that makes me feel a little lonely though. I live alone, my parents are gone. The old community is gone. On Christmas night I am going to have a big beautiful tree, a tasty Christmas goose, all kinds of kuchen, and all in a big empty house. Maybe it's not just young people who don't have a community to belong to."

"Well, Felix, it's up to you and me, a couple of old Krauts, to make a community happen this Christmas."

"Father, you are invited to dinner."

"Felix, I accept. *Danke schoen.*"

"Five O'clock Christmas Day. So, *bitte schoen.*"

"So *danke schoen.* Oh, Felix, I almost forgot. There are all kinds of things going on here. Can you organize these things on the back table?"

With that the back door opened up and Fr. Tom O'Gorman, a personality larger than life, came into the sacristy.

"*Guten tag, Hochwurdigen Pfarrer,* Good afternoon, Most Venerable Father," Fr. O'Gorman said to Father von Ackerman in perfect German.

Fr. Van Ackerman smiled warmly. You could tell immediately they liked each other.

"Herr Felix, how are you this afternoon?" and before waiting for a reply, he went on, "You guys, my head is spinning from all the events this month in this one little place. Felix, I'll have to help lay all this stuff out in the back of church. So before we go out here's what we've got. Guadalupe candles are for sale on the back table until December 11th. We have a flyer about the Guadalupe mass with the mariachis on December 12th. We have the <u>oplatki/ oblaten</u> wafers for sale for the Poles and the Germans. The Germans have a *Kris Kindlmarkt* next Sunday- selling Christmas cards and German ornaments and other little *chachkis* for the benefit of the S.O.S. Children's Villages in Austria. Here is sign-up sheet for the Americans for the-adopt a needy child Christmas gifts. There is a flyer about ticket sales for the Parish Christmas Brunch with Santa. And if that is not enough there is a sign-up sheet for La Paranda, when the Puerto Rican choir goes from house to house on Christmas Eve night to sing *villancicos*, Christmas carols. Oh, yes, and the Latino Charismatic group is calling all its members to participate in the *Sonríe, Jesús Te Ama* program. *Doña* Lidia Cruz has already started working Armitage Avenue."

Felix's eyes just widened at all the scheduled activity for so many different communities. All he could muster to say, "Boy, Father, this community has changed. It's not the old German community it used to be."

"Felix, we have so many immigrants from so many places in this city today, and in this parish. And so many young people! And they all seem to me like their searching for some glimpse of a welcoming community, for a kind word of welcome from somebody in a city that can be pretty cold and grey in December."

Father von Ackerman nodded and said. "I was telling Felix it was up to him and me, and of course, you, too, Father, to help make community and welcome happen. And we were saying how our old German Christmas traditions helped our parents and their generation feel at home in this country."

Father O'Gorman added, "When I look at all the events we are creating here, I know it is exhausting." He rolled his eyes into an exhausted look. "But I figure in the middle of this city if we can just create a place where people can at least feel at home for Christmas, we're doing something right."

"Father, on Christmas Day, I will have a beautiful tree, and a wonderful meal in a big empty house. I am sure you are busy, or may have family, but any time after five o'clock you are most welcome."

"Why, Felix, thank you. I was planning a quiet dinner with my mother, and my aunt who just lost her husband."

"Please bring them to dinner."

"Thank you, Felix, I will do that. That will be just great. Uh, Felix, I don't want to be pushy but I might need to bring along one or two other people, if that would not be a problem. My mother says I bring home every stray cat. But I can't help it sometimes at Christmas."

"Just let me know, Father."

Fr. O'Gorman swooped out of the sacristy. Fr. Von Ackerman paused for a moment and looked at Felix. He smiled and said, "Felix, I told you it's up to us two old Krauts to make a community, to bring people home for Christmas. I have a feeling a lot of people will be home for Christmas this year." He then slipped out the back door.

Felix spent the next hour getting the back tables in Church set up with the whole range of Christmas events, and national customs. About an hour later, the Church doors opened.

A youngish very dignified man stuck only his head in the door at first. "Hello?" Hearing nothing he inserted his whole body through the door. "Hello?"

188

Felix stepped around to face the door, "Hello, can I help you?"

"Yes. Can you tell us about this church?"

"Well, this is St. Monica's Church. It is a Catholic church."

"Who is the pastor? Is he around just now?"

"I'm sorry he just left. You might catch him at the rectory next door."

"Well, we are just so intrigued to find out about this place," said the stranger. The stranger went on, "The sign on your front lawn says Happy Chanukah! We never saw such a thing before."

Felix himself was intrigued and responded, "Oh, that is our pastor. He always says, 'Felix, everyone must be welcome.' I guess he wants to be sure the Jewish community will feel welcome too.".

"I need to meet this priest, "the stranger said. "Where can I find him?"

"In the rectory next store, I believe."

"Thank you. Oh, I'm sorry, I am Rabbi Seller. And I have never seen a sign like that on a Church before. I want to invite your pastor to our congregation."

The people with the rabbi nodded in agreement.

"Rabbi, it is an honor to meet you. If you have things to put out here for our community, let us know."

Just as the five-thirty mass was about to begin a frail old Latina lady came and stood in the back of the church. Felix had seen her around before but did not know her. He smiled at her, and she smiled back at him, and she said, "*Sonríe, Jesus te ama.*" And then in heavily accented English, "Smile, Jesus, loves you."

Felix remembered this must be the lady Fr. O'Gorman had spoken about. He went over and said, "Hello, my name is Felix."

The frail old lady smiled, but it was the shy smile of a young woman. It was almost disarming. Again in accented English, she spoke, "My name is Lydia Cruz. I go to the *Carismática aquí,* in dis Church. I tell all the people Jesus love them. Too many people looks too sad."

"Yes, you are right about that," said Felix.

With that, Lupe Parra, who was standing nearby listening in, interrupted, "*Doña* Lidia, how are you? *¿Qué haces?*"

Doña Lidia's face changed from the shy girlish smile to that of a *mujer determinada,* a determined woman.

"Lupe, les digo a todos que Jesus les ama. Es mi mission. *Desde el retiro yo sé que hay que mostrar el amor de Cristo en todas formas. Pues, soy vieja. No tengo dinero para dar limosnas. Ya se murieron mi hija and mi nieta y no tengo nadie para cuidarles bien. Y yo veo tanta gente aquí que les me parecen muy tristes. Por eso voy donde quiera, al tren, a la* food *store, aquí en la avenida de las tiendas. Y les digo solamente, el poco inglés que conozco: Jesus loves you. Y algunas me sonreían. Y eso vale todo. Otros me miran como*

si fuera una loquita, pero ni modo. El Señor los quiere. Y este es lo que les digo."

"*Doña* Lidia, that's beautiful, said Lupe"

"What did the lady say, ma'am?"

"Oh, my name is Lupe. She is *Doña* Lidia Cruz."

"Pleased to meet you. I am Felix Muench, a long time parishioner."

"Well, *Doña* Lidia told me she was troubled because she sees so many sad people in our neighborhood, especially young people. She says that she is old now, her daughter and grandchild died, so she is alone, but she is not sad, because she knows Jesus loves her. She wants to tell everybody that so they don't feel sad and alone. So she goes to the el station, to the food stores and other places to share that message."

"Well, that is beautiful", said Felix.

"Yes, but she said she goes to the El station and stands at the bottom of the stairs. Sometimes she stands in front of the super market. She tells people Jesus loves them. She said some people think she is just a crazy old lady, but she says it is her mission."

"Well, God bless her", said Felix, and then turned to *Doña* Lidia, and raising his voice as though that would help with the language barrier, he took her hand and said very loudly," God bless you."

Doña Lidia grinned, and that girlish smile returned.

In the following weeks, Felix did not alter his Saturday routine. He was at the Church by 3:00 p.m. and he ushered the 5:30 p.m. mass. One Saturday before Christmas he recognized his next door neighbors. He had not ever spoken to them in the several years they had lived next store.

Tim and Ellen Masterson were what they used to call Yuppies; young professional and upwardly mobile. They had purchased the three flat next to Felix's home. They rehabbed hit and turned it into a single family residence. Felix had observed all of this. They seemed busy about many things but not the kind of people looking to make friends of their neighbors.

But Felix thought about Fr. Von Ackerman, "Us old Krauts have to make a community here." So he went over and introduced himself to Tim and Ellen.

Tim said they had been out shopping and had been looking for a real Christmas tree.

Tim added, "I'm from Michigan originally and we've always had a real tree. But, boy, it's tough to find a good one in the city."

Felix smiled, "In my family we have always had a real tree. We are old fashion Germans. I just got my tree. I get it from the same place every year and they deliver it."

Tim was incredulous, "Really? Where?"

"From Denziger nursery out in Mundelein. They might still have a tree or two. I can bring their number over when I get home if you like."

"That would be great!"

Ellen had been dropping off the Krist Kindl gifts, and rejoined Tim.

"Honey, this is Felix Muench, our next store neighbor. Felix, this is my wife Ellen." Ellen just smiled, as though she needed to move on.

Felix said, "I am very happy to meet you."

"Honey,' Tim added, "Felix knows where we can, well maybe at this late date, get a real Christmas tree....and they deliver it." Ellen seemed more interested in Felix all of a sudden.

Then she got a look of disdain on her face, and said, "Tim, there's that crazy lady from in front of the food store. I didn't know she came here, too."

Felix stepped in, "Oh, that is *Doña* Lidia Cruz. She has suffered a lot in life. She lost her daughter and grandchild last year. But she still feels that she is blessed and that God loves her. She told me a few weeks back that she thinks so many people in our neighborhood look sad and unhappy, and she says it is her mission to try to cheer them up and remind them that no matter how bad it is God loves them."

"Huh", was Ellen's response. But it was the kind of "huh" that came from somewhere deep and rather than disdain it conveyed admiration.

Tim just said," Wow."

Ellen stood looking at *Doña* Lidia and then said, "You know some friends of ours were coming from work last week, and that same lady was at the bottom of the El station and telling everybody Jesus loves you. They thought she was crazy, too. Tim, remember, Cathy O'Brien just went on and on about the crazy old Latino lady. She said she was like a crazy bag lady or something. But, wow, that takes some courage for an old lady to act on her beliefs like that."

In the weeks before Christmas Felix was on hand as the Mexicans celebrated *las posadas,* the welcoming of the holy family, pilgrims, like most of the immigrant people in the hall. There were piñatas, and tamales and atole in the church hall. For Poles and Germans, *oplatki/ oblaten* wafers sold like hot cakes. For the Puerto Ricans everything was readiness for La Paranda.

As people left each event, there was *Doña* Lidia: "Jesus loves you."

And there was Felix, "Us old Krauts have to create Gemeinschaft, the community."

On Christmas Eve, Felix was again the usher at the 5:00 p.m. mass. This gave him all the time he would need to prepare for the Christmas dinner. In the intervening weeks he had invited Lupe Parra and *Doña* Lidia Cruz for dinner. He didn't think it right they should be alone. Fr. Von Ackerman called to say he had an old friend who was a missionary priest who would be in town visiting. Fr. O'Gorman confirmed that he was bringing his mother and his aunt, and he had two more surprise guests.

Felix was sitting at home before going off to church and said out loud to nobody, "I still have a lot of food. I may go out to the byways and highways, like it says in the bible."

194

As he was handing out the music programs for the Christmas Eve mass, Felix was standing next to Fr. O'Gorman when two women came in together. One was holding a two month old baby boy. With them was also an older woman.

"Felix, you know Jana and Debbie, they own the women's bookshop down the street. And this is their son, Eric. But we all call him Rocky."

Jana added, "And Father this is my mother, Elsa Reinmann. She is up from downstate."

After Father greeted Mrs. Reinmann, Felix added, "That sounds like a good German name. I am Felix Muench."

Mrs. Reinmann's face lit up and said, "*Ja, echtes deutsch,* my mother and father came from Germany."

"Mine, too," added Felix, from Ilerthyssen, near the Schwarzwald."

"Oh my God, I can't believe it! My parents came from Elsgau not too far from Ilerthyssen."

"Well. Welcome home," grinned Felix.

"I came to see my grandson. You know, I don't know about all these new things. I mean my daughter and her friend…"

"But we all love baby Rocky, Elsa."

Felix just added, "*Frohe Weinachten!*" Elsa grinned and bowed her head in that formal German nod.

After the reading of the Christmas story, the Fr. O'Gorman stepped down out of the pulpit and came down into the congregation. He looked around for a moment, and spotted Jana, Debbie and the baby.

"What a beautiful baby!" said the priest pointing with both hands toward Rocky. "May I borrow him for a moment?"

Jana was protective but the priest was there in front of her, "What a beautiful baby!" He repeated and he leaned over and blessed the baby. He whispered, "I'll be careful with him."

Jana let the priest take the baby. He then held the baby up for all to see,

"Didn't I tell you this was a beautiful baby! How could anybody but love him? Want to hold him? Want to care for him? Who could ever be afraid of a baby so beautiful and tender?" he handed Rocky back to Jana. "Do you see this baby? Do you understand that tonight God is trying to show us he loves us so much? We are not afraid of this baby, but sometimes we are afraid of God, and too often afraid of each other. So, tonight God says again: look at this baby, this is me! This is how I come to you. Open your arms to me! Open your hearts to me! A baby born to a virgin comes to us tonight so that we might open our hearts to God. The gospel says, 'he dwelt among us and made his home with us'…and later on…'Love following upon love.' 'This is what God wants for us. This is what we crave for our lives and each other…that love follow upon love.'"

The deepest truth of this message was not lost on Jana, nor her mother, nor Debbie her partner, nor even the preacher. Everyone had tears running down their faces. Lupe Parra watching also thought, "the innocent child of the lesbian mother, this is how God is reaching out to us all tonight."

Tears filled her eyes as well.

When the service was over, the pastor stood at the back of the church wishing all Merry Christmas! *Frohe Weinachten! Wesolych Swiat! Feliz Navidad!*

And one step further stood *Doña* Lidia Cruz: "Jesus loves you!"

Felix was again talking to Elsa Reinmann, as Jana, Debbie and baby Rocky looked on.

Out of the corner of his eye, Felix spotted Fr. Von Ackerman. They exchanged glances and grinned at each other.

"Elsa, you know at my home tomorrow night we will have a traditional German Christmas dinner. Everything is all ready. I would love to have you and your family come and join us. Fr. O'Gorman is coming and Fr. Von Ackerman, and some other wonderful people, too."

"Oh, we couldn't impose."

"No, no, it is no imposition. There is so much food, please come all of you. Besides I want to hear more about your shop. We had a jewelry store here in the neighborhood for many, many years."

Elsa looked at Jana, who turned to Debbie. Felix added, "So kleine Eric, I mean Rocky, can have a real German first Christmas."

It was Jana who finally said, "Okay, why not, thank you." She could see how delighted her mother was at the prospect of an old fashioned German Christmas. It would be like going home.

On Christmas morning, Felix was running some things out to the garbage in the alley. He ran into Tim Masterson. "Merry Christmas, Felix!"

"Merry Christmas, Tim. Did you get the tree?"

"We did indeed, Felix, we can't thank you enough."

"I thought you were heading up to Michigan for Christmas Day."

"Well, we were. But my folks called last night to warn us that there is a huge blizzard hitting up there today. We decided it was a better idea to head up tomorrow."

"Well, then, I hope you and Ellen will please come over for dinner. I have a lot of food. It is a big traditional German Christmas dinner. The parish priests are coming over, and a lot of other people you may know. We are just going to make our own Christmas community tonight."

"Let me check with Ellen to make sure she didn't make other plans already."

When dinner time finally came, Felix's house was filled with people. The Masterson's came. *Doña* Lidia and Lupe Parra came. Fr. Von Ackerman and his missionary friend came. Elsa and Jana and Debbie and baby Rocky came. Fr. O'Gorman came with his mother and his aunt, and his surprise guests: Rabbi Seller and his wife.

As the gathered folks were digging into their *Johannesbeer Sahne Torte*, there came a sound from outside. It was La Paranda, the Puerto Rican choir was making a stop out in front. Everyone in Felix's house went out on the porch and suddenly a very upbeat island rhythm started, and the choir sang: "*Palomita Blanca, Palomita blanca, del piquito azul, quiero que me lleve a ver a Jesu*". Everybody was moving, elbows, arms and hips.

Ellen just began to laugh out loud, and Tim was grinning from ear to ear. "God, this is wild. It's like here comes everybody," he said.

Tim said to Ellen, "Look at this group. Then he began to softly hum an old Christmas song to Ellen, "*I'll be home for Christmas.*"

Ellen answered. "Looks like everybody's home this Christmas."

Made in the USA
Columbia, SC
09 June 2019